GIRL SPOKEN FOR

SUZIE T. ROOS

This book is a work of fiction. Names, characters, places, and incidents are the product of the author's imagination or are used fictitiously. Any resemblance to actual events, locales, or persons, living or dead, is coincidental.

Girl Spoken For
Copyright © 2010, Copyright © 2015 by Suzie T. Roos

All rights reserved. No part of this book may be reproduced or transmitted in any form or by any means, electronic or mechanical, including photocopying, recording, or by any information storage and retrieval system, without permission in writing from the publisher.

Cover Photo Photographed, Backdrop Painting and Body Art by Leroy Roper.
Model and Costuming by Tiffany Diamond
Art Direction by Suzie T. Roos

Cover Design and Interior format by The Killion Group
http://thekilliongroupinc.com

To the one person who I can always count on. The one person who accepts my adventures and embraces them with me. To the one who stole my heart at fifteen years of age. The one I call husband.

CHAPTER 1

January 5, 1989

I felt less and less like myself in the weeks following my grandmother's death.
 Jumpy. Moody. Reclusive. Definitely not the Tatum Duncan everyone knew.

I was numb to the world most days, which was not a challenge in St. Louis in early February. The earth was dead-looking in its dormant state, waiting for spring flowers. While most kids prepared for spring break, I kept agonizing over how I was going to live the rest of my life without the person who'd been my best friend.

Grandma was the one person I could tell my deepest secrets to. She understood me. And never in my life had I gone a week, let alone two weeks, without talking to her. Until now.

After many calls from my friends failed to get me out of my bedroom, where I brooded about the death of my grandmother, they began to call less. My bedroom had become a private sanctuary. And that suited me just fine.

So as usual, I was happy to escape to school Monday morning. That is, until the school bully, Neville ("Neville the Devil"), sat behind me in sixth hour. The last thirty seconds before the bell rang gave him just enough time to start in on me. I could feel his breath in my hair.

"Come on, Tate-eeee . . . how 'bout a quickie after class."

Typically I could ignore Neville, but not this day.

When the bell rang announcing the end to sixth hour, I spit in his face and hauled ass out of the classroom.

"Get back here, bitch," he shouted in the hall.

Neville rushed up behind me and flipped me to the floor, then laughed. Maybe it was funny to watch me flail like a goldfish on the hallway floor. But I was more worried about the contents of my purse that spewed out in clear view. *Crap.* Lip gloss. Canker sore melts. Tampons. Still on the floor, I scrambled, shoving them back in my purse.

Neville laughed. "Guess you won't be spreading your legs this week."

That did it!

By the time I reached the front door of my house, the high school principal had called my mom about the "quarrel" with Neville. I couldn't even get inside before World War III broke out in my living room.

With no defense, I collapsed on the couch, stared at my hands in my lap, and avoided Mom's glare. Like a dog, she'd interpret my stare as a challenge.

Her pacing reminded me of the Road Runner on a three-day caffeine binge. Her need to control everyone had given me ulcers before I'd had my first menstrual period.

"Tatum Frances, you know I don't like telling people our business. But I had to make the principal understand why you flipped your damn lid. We all know how hard it is right now with Granny gone. We all miss her, but do you see me or your father slugging people in the groin because they said something stupid or ignorant to us?" Mom spun around, appearing to need an oxygen mask.

"Cynthia, calm down," Dad said, following Mom into the living room, aka the Roman Coliseum.

Mother gave my father the if-you-want-to-keep-breathing look. "Look at the way she dresses. People look at her funny. Who wears combat boots with miniskirts? And now she's fighting boys? Kenny, what did I say would happen if she spent all of her free time with your mom? Now, look, she can barely function without her. Young girls aren't best friends with their grandmothers—"

My heart bungee-jumped up to my throat. Would hearing my mother say I was a freak ever get easier?

"It's not normal. And talking about normal . . . from here on out, you're going to stop wearing those stupid ripped up-clothes and dress normal. And you're going out with Christy or Diane this weekend. Pick one. They both called a million times last weekend alone."

Mom was right about one thing. It was stupid of me to alienate the people I could talk to. I needed to call Christy and Diane.

Dad crossed his arms over his chest, muscles flexing. "Enough. Tatum is respectable, no matter what she wears. Her friends understand what she's going through right now. They're good girls."

I had enough of Mom making me feel worse than I already did. "But I'd be more respectable if I dressed like Sandra Dee?" Time to drive the dagger home.

"Grandma didn't mind how I dressed. She always said I looked grown-up."

Mom had always been jealous of how close I was to my dad's mother. And those words were surely going to strike her pride. Not my fault my mom never learned how to express her emotions or feelings and my grandmother did it every day of her life—we had that in common.

"Stop, Tatum," Dad said, clearly cutting off any retaliation Mom was about to load onto me. "The point is we know damn well what that principal said."

"Dad, what did he say?"

He sat next to me on the couch and lightly patted my shoulder. "He said you're a good student, and basically, this kid isn't. He sounds really violent. Lucky he didn't hit you, Tate."

I hadn't given Neville a chance to hit me, but having his reputation reiterated made me realize how badly the situation could have gone.

"That's not the point," Mother spat. "Fighting at school will ruin your record with a suspension. That means goodbye to any scholarship money. You're a sophomore . . . two more lousy years, and you're going to blow it because someone called you a name. Tell you what" —Mother's pointer finger trembled faster than a double bass drum—"we'll wait and see what the principal says tomorrow, but if you get suspended we'll . . . we'll . . . put you in Maryville."

Dad leaped from the couch. "Don't be ridiculous. One fight does not equal Maryville."

"What's Maryville?" My voice cracked.

Dad looked back at me, relaxing his frown lines. "It's a ho—school for troubled girls. Don't worry, you're not going there. But go to your room. I wanna talk to your mother."

Oh, no . . . she can't send me away. If Grandma was here she would offer to have a talk with Mom to save me. Maybe that's exactly what I deserve, though, to be sent away. Because I'll never be the kind of daughter she wants. Never.

I kept board straight, not wanting her to see me quiver. In the living room doorway, I glanced back at Dad. He nodded, reassurance written all over his face.

Wimpy of me to let Dad calm Mom down. Especially after I struck back at her twice, one more strike and she'd release Hades on me. She lives by the three-strike rule. Maybe I should've kept my mouth shut. Why chance her grounding me for a week or two just so I could make my point, because she would never see my point. She'd just say I was popping off to her.

Hours later my baby sister, Toni, knocked on the bedroom door before bedtime. "Tatey, can Gizzi and I come in?"

"Of course, Tone."

Toni and Gizmo—our Jack Russell terrier—came in and quickly stretched out on my bed.

"Mommy's still mad, Tatey. What happened?" asked my five-year-old mouse of a sister.

We were ten years apart, but no matter, I knew Toni needed someone to relate to her. My mom wasn't capable of relating to either of her children. I'd been lucky enough to have my grandma for almost sixteen years.

I sat down next to Toni and wrapped my arm around her little shoulder. "Nothing that justifies this. Don't worry, it'll be okay." Whether I believed it or not was another question. "You have a bedtime story for me to read you?"

Toni's eyes lit up. "I do." She ran to my nightstand and grabbed her favorite story—*Pippi Longstocking*. She climbed back in bed, snuggling her tush next to me. "Pippi's funny." Her innocent eyes stared up at me. "Grandmee said it's good to be different. And we're different . . . right, Tatey?"

Hmm. Curious. Pippi wore black boots and crazy stockings with skirts. This was the perfect story for Toni. "You betchya! No matter what anyone says, it's okay to be different."

The next morning I wasn't sure where I'd rather be—home or school. Neither option felt sane.

It didn't help any that when I met Christy at the bus stop, she stood near me, but didn't talk. If Christy didn't have much to say . . . things were bad.

"Hey, Chris, I was going to call you last night but got busy." Busy getting threatened to be put in an all-girls home.

Her shaped eyebrows shot upward. "Ohh . . ."

This wasn't going to be easy. I had to take a deep breath. "Yeah. I need to apologize for pushing you away recently. It's just . . . with my grandma gone now . . . I'm sorry. Am I forgiven?"

Christy flung her lanky arms around me. "Oh, you're crazy. Of course." She backed away and held my shoulders. Her eager spirit was back in her big almond shaped eyes. "This weekend, we go out. Watch a movie at my house, or whatever you want to do is fine with me. Okay?"

"Of course. This weekend, it's a date."

One obstacle down, a bigger one to go. They would page me the moment the bell rang for first hour. So when our bus pulled up in front of the brick box they called Randall High School, it took all my strength to walk in there.

At least I was prepared when the intercom clicked on, requesting my immediate presence in the principal's office. This was it.

The route to the principal's office would be a long and lonely walk. But I wasn't alone. Zach Bertano was in the hall and headed straight for me. Zach, the loner guy every girl wanted but no one could get close to. We were friends, but he never asked me to do anything with him. He was just a "school friend"—a hot school friend. He was tall and slender. Not to mention I had a thing for guys with Johnny Cash black hair and onyx eyes. His smile was the only bright thing in my life at the moment.

Zach was "different."

"Hey, Tate, I heard you got paged." He stepped up to me.

His brightness warmed my soul like hot cocoa going down.

"Why did you take on 'Neville the Devil' by yourself yesterday? Then you skipped last period. What's going on? Are you okay?"

I couldn't breathe. Zach knew how to make me feel cared for. "I'm fine. And trust me, I'd rather have been in class than walking all the way home."

He had one of those infectious laughs. "You walked? If I'd known, I could have driven you. That's a long way. Now, tell me why you attacked Neville. What did he do this time?"

What girl thinks she can impress a guy by telling him she went postal on a jerk who asked for a blow job? "Plain and simple, he wasn't a gentleman. And I've had . . . well, kind of a bad couple of weeks. I just wasn't thinking straight. So here I am."

He stepped closer, looking down at me. "I heard about your grandma—I'm real sorry, Tatum. I know how much she meant to you."

It would have been easier if he'd stepped on my toes, but instead, Zach had to deal the "I care" card.

The intercom clicked on. "Tatum Duncan, *immediately* report to the main office."

I started to shake, knowing my life had come down to one decision. Dear god, my mother was right. It was over for me.

One suspension. Zero scholarships. Equaled Maryville.

The heater must have clicked on. The cami under my mom's favorite poodle sweater from her high school days stuck to my body. When I'd asked her to wear her old sweater this morning it made her unreasonably happy, and she'd eagerly handed it over. Little did she know I'd planned on wearing it with a miniskirt and the combat boots she hated so much.

I adjusted my skirt and sweater. "Guess they're looking for me. See ya, Zach."

"Wait. I'll go with you."

I paused, looking back to examine his face. He was serious.

"Why? For what?"

He kept walking, passing me. "Because you may need me. Let's go."

"Need you? How?" I jogged to catch up. "Why would you want to come? This is gonna get ugly. And quick."

"It won't if I can help it." Zach held the office door for me. "Don't worry."

We didn't say a word to each other. Best not to, since I wanted to ask if he'd lost his mind.

He stayed next to me, not touching, but close. We were friends, but why was he doing this? How could he help me? I was bound for suspension. Couldn't he see that?

The principal's secretary noticed us standing there. "Can I help you?"

"Hi. I'm Tatum Duncan. I was paged."

"Finally. Yes, Mr. Johnson is waiting for you." She looked at Zach. "But why are you here, Mr. Bertano?"

She knew his name? She didn't know mine. How many times had he been to the principal's office?

"I'm here because Tatum needs a witness."

I jerked my head up. *Witness?*

He was cool. I was so not.

The secretary lowered her eyes and grinned. "I see." She picked up her phone. "Mr. Johnson, Miss Duncan is here with a witness." The smirk on her face said she couldn't believe what she was saying. That made two of us.

Zach stood there as if he were the President of the United States—and he didn't expect to wait. At least, not long.

"Yes, I said 'a witness.' It's Mr. Bertano." The secretary whispered, looking away, "The youngest one."

"What are you doing?" I mumbled to Zach.

He didn't move. "Shh. You'll see."

Not sure why I trusted him, but I envied his confidence. But I had no clue why he dared get involved with this situation.

The secretary hung up the phone. "You two may go in." She waved her arm toward the first door on the left, behind her.

They were allowing him in there with me? This had to be a dream—a bad one.

Zach stepped ahead of me and pushed the door open.

"Miss Duncan, have a seat." The approaching principal pointed to one of the two chairs in front of his desk.

I quickly sat, knowing my legs would give out soon.

This is it. Here it comes. Suspension. I've never even had detention. Damn it.

The door closed and Zach took the seat next to me.

Mr. Johnson took his plush leather chair. His hands folded on top of his desk. "Miss Duncan, I'm aware of your situation at home."

Wonderful. Now he'd make me cry. And I didn't want Zach to see me like that. Not sure why, but I never wanted anyone to see me as weak. Possibly Mom had something to do with that. Possibly.

Mr. Johnson's jaw tightened. "I'm sorry, but fighting isn't allowed in this school. We don't take violence lightly. Especially punching someone in their groin area."

My hand twitched, knowing the principal was working up to announce my punishment—suspension. I tucked my hands under my legs. "Yes, sir. I know, and I apologize."

Zach shifted his weight in the seat. "Mr. Johnson, what Tatum isn't saying is how she's teased and taunted in that class. Even after the bell rang, Neville ran after her. He grabbed her by the collar and flipped her to the floor. Tatum had to defend herself at that point. And she did."

I was a mess. My life had turned into a scrambled Rubik's Cube. "Zach, it's fine."

He faced me. "No, Tatum. He needs to know what happened."

What was more shocking was that Mr. Johnson let Zach continue. I continued to be as useful as a broken paper clip holding a stack of papers.

Mr. Johnson lounged back in his chair. "Kind of what I suspected. Tatum, I've examined your record and it's clean. But Mr. Bertano, you're not in that class with her. How do you know what took place?"

"I've heard about the bullying Tatum gets during that period from others. And I personally saw Neville chase her down the hall after the bell. I just couldn't get there fast enough."

Looking at Zach beside me made my tightened chest loosen. If only he'd look at me so I could see his eyes. He was so serious. Not that this wasn't serious—it was, but it was a bit awkward to have them talk about me as if I weren't sitting next to them.

"I see. So Miss Duncan, please tell me what Neville said in class." We were finally back to the punishment. *Just get this over with.*

I had to take a breath to calm down. My heart was racing down the football field. "The usual, sir. Calling me names. Making fun of me. Things about sex."

Mr. Johnson leaned forward. "Neville has been expelled for the remainder of the year. I know it's tough for you at home right now. So we'll ignore this one incident. But, if there is a next time, you'll be suspended. Focus on keeping your grades up. And again, Miss Duncan, I'm sorry about your grandmother. My secretary will give you both a hall pass."

We were excused, no consequence. I almost fell over from disbelief, but happy disbelief.

Since Zach and I had the same class, we walked together.

Once we were out in the hall, I turned to him. "Zach, just tell me one thing. Why did you do that for me?"

"You would have sat there and let the principal give you detention or suspend you for protecting yourself against Neville. Neville would have hurt you if you hadn't stopped him. And I wasn't about to see you take the rap for sticking up for yourself. Besides, any guy who attacks a girl isn't someone I want around. Especially around you." He glanced at me, but just long enough for our eyes to meet.

The crash-test dummy hit a brick wall. My heart stopped. My jaw snapped open.

Zach kept walking away.

Did he not realize what he'd said to me? Forget why Zach insisted on going to the principal's office, but he didn't want a violent guy around *me*? Why did he care so much?

"Come on, Tatum. We're already late. Move those combat boots of yours."

CHAPTER 2

Since I wasn't being shipped to an all-girls home, and wasn't even grounded, I kept my word to Christy and went to her house Saturday for movie night.

Eric, her new boyfriend, joined us. If he weren't a surfer, laid-back type of guy, I would have felt uncomfortable being the third wheel, but I didn't.

An hour after I got to her house, her doorbell rang. Christy and Eric both had enormous Mick Jagger smiles on their faces and stared at me.

Christy put her popcorn down on the coffee table and sauntered to her front door, calling out, "Coming."

When the door opened, I didn't need to see the guy's face to know who it was. I knew his voice. Christy and Eric had conveniently not mentioned that they'd invited Kyle Wilson. He was a sophomore like us, but he was the newest, hottest rising football star at Randall High. Not to mention, he had a face chiseled to perfection and a body that could be used to advertise strong athletic wear.

I immediately looked down at my clothes. Crap. I hadn't even showered after school.

Christy and Kyle walked in. I ignored Christy since she was gloating like a buffoon. My attention remained on Kyle and his strong jaw, strong shoulders . . . strong everything. One deep breath and I swore my body sank through the couch.

Christy sat down next to Eric. "Tatum, you know Kyle. Kyle, you know Tate."

Kyle tossed his hand up and half waved. "Hi. We met last year in literature. Mrs. Shrimp's class."

"Yeah, I think that's right."

Kyle took the seat next to me on the couch. He hadn't taken his eyes off of me, not once. And his smile was contagious. I was sure I wasn't looking as cool and confident as Kyle.

"So, Christy said it's movie night. You don't mind if I join you guys?"

Holy crap. This isn't happening. Kyle Wilson, who can have any girl he wants, asked to hang out with us? With me*?*

I moved to scoot away, but stopped. "Of course not." My breathing was unpredictable. I had to calm down.

Christy started the movie and flipped the light switch off. Kyle slid closer to me on the couch. And all I could think about was my personal hygiene. Or lack thereof.

The four of us grew closer in just two weeks.

One afternoon at Christy's house, I asked her if we could speak privately. Christy and I walked far enough down her driveway so the guys would need bionic hearing to spy on us.

"So, do you know what's going on with Kyle? I thought he liked me. I mean, he's been exclusively hanging out with us, instead of the team, but he hasn't said anything about being more than friends." Kyle and I flirted with each other daily. And if he didn't plan on asking me to date him, then why not hang out with the team? Was he toying with me?

"Oh, come on, Tatum. You know he likes you," she replied with a reassuring grin.

"Well, I thought he did, but . . ."

"Look. Don't stress. Kyle does want you to go out with him. He's just looking for the right time to ask you." A naughty expression spread across her face. "A varsity football player wants ya, Tate."

How did she get that information? Was it true?

She took my hands, hopping like my baby sister did when she got to go to Chuck E. Cheese's. "This'll be soo fun. You and me both dating jocks, how cool is that? We'll double date!"

I'd originally wanted him to ask me to be his girlfriend, but the moment Christy confirmed that he was interested, I panicked. Kyle was intimating. I was definitely not his type. He was the big guy at school. I mean, the really big, cute hunk of a guy.

"Why hasn't he said anything to me? He's had chances, but not a single word," I said. Kyle had to know I'd never dated anyone. Shoot. I'd never even kissed a boy. Of course, he wouldn't know *that*. "I mean, he's cool and all, but what do we have in common? Not football. And we all know I'm not a cheerleader."

Surprisingly, her large eyes got bigger. "Who cares if you're not a cheerleader, you idiot? Don't you know a good thing when it smacks you upside your head? Huh? Stop making excuses." A sly grin spread across her face. "You're scared."

Christy knew the truth and it made my stomach churn with sour milk. "You're crazy. I'm not scared." At least, I wouldn't admit that to her.

"Don't try to play dumb, Tatum Duncan. Not with me. I see it all over your face. You're scared of dating. Dating a popular guy. Uh huh, that's it. But fine. Whatever. You're just missing out . . . *again.*" Christy flipped her Farrah Fawcett hair over her shoulder and left me standing there.

But then she stopped, turned, and looked me square in the eye. "You know, it might actually do you some good to get a boyfriend, Tatum."

"Oh, really now. Why is that?"

"Since your grandma died, you haven't been yourself. I'm sorry. I know things are hard right now, but if it weren't for Kyle, you'd still be a hermit in that bedroom of yours. This is your chance to be normal again. And for the love of god, stop ripping your fishnets."

Maybe Christy was right. Maybe I needed a change. Maybe dating the star football player was the answer. There was no denying it was fun when Kyle took me to dinner at the mall.

Kyle seemed to be with Christy and me more and more often at school.

I noticed positive attention went where Kyle and I did. His football buddies always greeted us together—Kyle and Tatum.

I didn't mind that, but something nagged at me. A nagging like the chores that waited for me at home. I could never predict what Kyle would do next. Despite how intuitive my grandmother had thought I was, I could never read Kyle right. Out of left field, he became very handsy, real fast. Kyle would rest his arm across my shoulders, close to my breast. I wasn't used to anyone touching me, let alone a hot guy. There were two things I noticed about his touching. First, he did this solely in Zach Bertano's presence. This was more obvious when Zach would give me a dirty look and slam his locker shut before storming off. Secondly, every time Kyle rested his arm around my shoulders, I thought he'd ask me to be his girlfriend. But he never did.

Days later, Christy and I joined Kyle in Eric's basement to watch a movie. When a commercial took over the screen, Christy and Eric bolted up the carpeted steps.

"Sorry. Where are they going?" I turned my head to Kyle.

Kyle scooted closer to me on the plaid couch, slid his arm over my shoulder, and dangled his hand above my breast.

"Will you go out with me?" Kyle blurted.

I couldn't believe that he'd asked. But he had. He'd finally asked me, Tatum Duncan, to go out with him. About frickin' time.

"So what do you say, will you be my girlfriend?"

"Sure." My tongue tripped, and that's all that came out. Then it happened . . . he leaned toward me.

Oh, no. I need to practice first. He's gonna notice I'm an amateur kisser.

I turned my head. My cheek got a wonderful kiss.

The goal was to keep my inexperience a secret. Thankfully, he accepted my cheek.

This situation was exactly what I feared about dating a guy with such status and experience when I had neither. Desperate times called for desperate measures; I'd have to practice on my teddy bear. *Sorry, Mr. Bigalow, but I need to start practicing the moment I get home.* It turned out okay, but that kiss could have been my *Titanic*.

No denying it, though, having an awesome boyfriend lit a bottle rocket inside me. Someone to show me love and affection. I wouldn't be so lonely. We could study together. He had to keep his grades up to stay on the team, and I had to keep mine up for scholarships.

Not that I was some schmuck, but dating Kyle could only improve my reputation.

CHAPTER 3

February 6, 1989

The following Monday at school, the student council had posted the decorations and invitations for the Sweetheart Dance all over the walls. This dance only meant problems for me. It was no secret what went on between guys and girls after school dances. With how "handsy" Kyle had already been toward me, this dance would be my boot camp.

At my locker, I noticed more commotion than usual. Eric and Christy were at her locker a couple of doors down from mine. They smiled and stared in my direction. This was becoming a sign—something was up.

Kyle stood against my locker door, but when I arrived, he scooted off to the side. "Morning, Tate."

"Hi, Kyle."

He brushed his hand along my shoulder. "I have a question for you."

"Sure." I didn't turn around while rearranging my books for the day.

"I wanted to talk to you about the dance."

Being a total prude wouldn't be easy to conceal from the rest of my class much longer. Once a football player finds out about your inexperience, the whole school finds out.

"Tate, the dance . . . we're going, right?"

I took a deep breath before saying, "You didn't really ask me."

"Tate, it's a given. You're my girlfriend." The corners of Kyle's lips were drawn down.

Hurting his feelings was not my intention. "'Course I'll go with you." I turned completely around to face him.

Kyle grabbed me and pulled my body to his chest. "Cool, we're going, then."

That evening my family was seated around the dining room table. Dad was shoveling scoops of spaghetti onto his plate. Mom placed her napkin over her lap. Toni loaded her plate with garlic bread and nothing else.

It was now or never. "Mom, Dad . . . today a guy asked me to the Sweetheart Dance."

Dad stopped feeding his face and sat back. Mom's back shot board straight. Toni stared at me. I began to dish my food, acting casual.

Mom responded. "This is sudden. Have we met him? I suppose you can go, that's not a problem. But what do we need to do?"

I twirled some spaghetti around my fork. "I don't think anything, Mom. I just need to get a dress." No one else talked.

"A dress? We can go shopping tonight!" Mom had always been a real dress junkie. The only reason to buy a dress was to make me look as she preferred—like Shirley Temple's sister.

"Tonight?" A solid head-butt to my calf—Gizmo was at my feet. I slid a piece of garlic bread under the table for him. Every dinner he was underneath the table, waiting for me to "accidently" drop some food. I made sure to always come through for my Gizmo.

"If you need one, we better grab one before they're all gone. The dance is this weekend, right? All right, Toni, finish up. We need to go soon. Tate, stop slouching at the dinner table. Sit up straight."

"Now tell me about this boy," Dad asked before taking another bite.

"What do you want to know?" Not much, I hoped, since I barely knew him. Dad swallowed, looking up at me. "I want to know what he's like. What's his thing . . . sports, cars, music? You know, stuff like that."

I coughed a giggle, "Well, not music." He had horrible taste in music. I took a moment to think of a nice attribute of Kyle's besides the fact that he was totally hot. "He's a football player."

Mom whipped around from the sink like I'd told her we won the lottery. "A football player? Well, why didn't you say that?"

For once, my mom was actually excited about something pertaining to me. "I didn't think it was that big of a deal. But he did try out for JV and made varsity."

Dad stopped eating and looked at me. "A sophomore like you?"

I nodded.

Dad's mouth rolled, showing he was impressed.

Mother smiled. "Is he tall?"

Dad jerked his head toward her. "Don't you mean, 'Is he nice?'"

Mom smacked her lips. "Of course I want to know that. But her dating a talented football player is nice. I never dated a football player."

Dad's eyes nearly popped out of his head. "No, you dated a boxer. Be happy with that."

"Anyway, he's taller than me. And he's nice."

"Everybody's taller than you, Tatey." Toni said.

"Won't you two be quite the sight? Joe Montana & little Jodie Foster." Mother giggled.

Her comparison was not cute to me. I looked nothing like Jodie Foster.

Mom ran around the kitchen, humming random tunes. It was nice to see her interested in something I was doing for a change. Whether it was my boyfriend or me, something relating to me had made her smile.

I was admiring my new dress hanging from the closet door that night when my mom walked in my bedroom.

"Tate, I've talked to your dad, and he decided to rent you a car, a limo, for this dance."

I was shocked. "A car? Why? Kyle drives."

"Tatum, when I was your age, I didn't have things like this. No gorgeous dresses. No fancy shoes. Not one lousy dance. Let us do this for you. Besides, I figured it's your first and who knows how many dances you'll get invited to . . . especially with a varsity football player?"

"Uh, true, I suppose." She couldn't help but hurt my feelings. "But it's not like a prom, or even homecoming. It's not that big of a deal. Are you and Dad sure?"

"Of course I'm sure. We need to make a good impression."

We? *What does she mean by* we? "Thanks, Mom. I guess I do need help."

That Friday, Diane stopped by my locker before last hour. You could see her coming a mile away, always wearing funky glasses that should have been kept back in the sixties. She had a collection of them. A long-strapped messenger bag in black leather was draped across her shoulder. Her older brother's jeans, cuffed up, slouched on her hips.

"Hey, Diane. New glasses?" I asked, grabbing my books.

She leaned her back against Christy's locker and said, "Yup. My dad's old ones. I had to pop the lenses out. That man was seriously blind."

I didn't mention that they were three sizes too big for her. "So, what's up? Any plans for tonight?" "Unfortunately, I haven't met Mister Right yet, so, nothing. How 'bout you?"

"Open. Shall I ink you in? Maybe you could spend the night?" I closed my locker.

"Sure. That would be great. My parents are out of town all weekend."

She wouldn't look at me, appearing to be preoccupied.

"Diane, are you okay? It seems like . . . well . . . you all right?"

Diane met my stare. "Are you going out with Kyle Wilson?"

"Yeah. Why do you ask?" I wasn't getting the same giddy reaction from Diane that I'd gotten from my other girlfriends.

"He's in my fourth hour and was going on and on about you all week. That's all."

"What do you mean 'going on and on' about me? Like how?"

Diane looked toward the other side of the hall. She brushed the bangs out of her eyes. Her lips were twisting in an unnatural way.

"Helloooo?"

She met my stare again. "You know. Like how much 'fun'"—Di expressed quotes with her fingers—"you guys have together."

It began . . . Could he be doing that to try and cover up that he hadn't even copped a feel? That had to be why. People would get the wrong idea about me, though. I didn't need that kind of reputation.

"Look, Tate, don't get mad. It wasn't bad. I was making sure he wasn't being—"

"Being disrespectful?" I leaned against the lockers, staring into space. Diane joined me. That's when movement across the hall caught my attention.

Zach Bertano's body mainly faced his locker, but he was looking back over his shoulder at me.

I half waved to him. "Hey, Zach."

Zach's eyes narrowed on me. He didn't respond. His jaw was clenched—he was clearly frustrated and disappointed about something. *Remember to focus. I gotta take my time to read him. Grandma always said the eyes and mouth will give it all away.* Our eyes made direct contact. *It's me. It can't be me. Why? He's totally pissed at me. He's so focused on my eyes. I know damn well what those eyes just said to me.* He whipped back around.

"It's okay, Tatum. Kyle was just bragging about you," Diane said.

Slam. We both jumped.

Zach stormed off down the hall.

After dinner, Diane came over and we went roller skating, something we hadn't done in many months. We used to skate all the time when things were less complicated.

We walked into Spinning Wheels. The music boomed and the lights twirled. It was going to be a great girls' night out.

Diane tossed her black Converse high-tops next to my combat boots in a locker. We laced our skates and darted toward the heavily lacquered wooden floor.

Many songs later, it was time for a soda break. We collected our drinks and popcorn from the pick-up window.

"So, Tate, you're going to the Sweetheart Dance with Kyle, then?" Diane asked, claiming the corner booth.

"Yeah . . . why?"

"No particular reason." She wouldn't look at me.

"Are you going to the dance tomorrow?"

"Nah. No one asked me."

"Oh." How could she not be asked? Not only was she beautiful—long black curly hair and naturally tanned skin—she was fun. "Well, you can come with me and Kyle. I'm sure there's still tickets left, and besides, we haven't seen each other much recently." I really wanted her to join me. There would be plenty of room in the limo. Besides . . .

Di chuckled. "Not sure Kyle would want extra company. Thanks anyway."

"Oh, right. I guess I need to ask him first, but I'm sure he wouldn't mind. Are you positive you don't want to go?" With her there, I wouldn't worry about being alone with him.

"I'm sure, thanks," she replied with a twisted grin. "I'm just glad to see you out again, having fun. It's been a long time."

Suddenly we both heard the violin intro to "Come on Eileen" by Dexys Midnight Runners. We looked at each other and smiled.

"Shall we?" I said, getting to my feet.

"We shall." She held her hand out to me.

Hand in hand, we skated as fast as we could back to the rink. We went around twice, doing some of our usual moves, but on the last turn around I bit the dust, and hard.

"Tatum . . . Tatum, oh my god, are you okay?"

I was flat on my back with my right leg twisted underneath me and my left leg straight out—spitting image of a tangled Stretch Armstrong doll. How could I possibly be all right?

Two hours later, I got home from the ER, my foot and ankle were wrapped in an ACE bandage.

My father helped me out of the van and up our front porch steps. Diane followed, carrying my stuff.

Mother flung open the front door. "Let me see ya, Tate."

"Cynthia, don't start," Dad said, guiding me over the threshold.

Mother put Ebenezer Scrooge's bitter face to shame. "I'm not starting anything. I just wanna see what she's going to look like for this dance tomorrow. I can't believe she does this when a football player offers to take her to a dance. Once in a lifetime . . ."

"What do you want to see, Mom? Huh?" Why couldn't she care about me for once, ask if I was okay? She always acted like she was the victim. As if I'd done this to ruin her weekend.

"Don't you get an attitude with me, young lady. How do you expect to go to this dance? I just knew it was too good to be true."

I looked at Diane with a can-you-adopt-me expression. I snapped my head back at my mother. "What do you mean? I'm still going to the dance. I'll just be on crutches, so what?"

"You're darn right you're going." Mom straightened her back. "Your father and I spent a lot of money on your stuff. The car. The dress. The shoes. The jewelry."

And don't forget the Miracle Bra! I turned my crutches so they aimed for my bedroom. "I know you did. I'm still going. Don't worry, your money won't be wasted."

Diane followed me and closed the bedroom door behind us.

"Tate, are you sure you can dance?"

"Who said anything about dancing? I can go without having to dance." I lay down on my bed, shoving two pillows under my foot. Diane helped. "What I'm really worried about is getting Kyle to keep his hands to himself. Now, that's something to worry about. And besides, you heard my mom." I snickered. "We got all this stuff for me. Just for me!"

Diane turned on my old seventeen-inch Zenith.

"Sorry, Di. I ruined tonight for us." Honestly, I was glad she was spending the night, though. It had been nice having a good friend with me in the ER.

Diane crawled in bed and snuggled up to me. "No worries. No matter what you screw up, I've always got your back." She began to chuckle. "Whether it's in a hospital or not, you are soo going to need me."

CHAPTER 4

Saturday, February 13, 1989

My strapless teal dress lay in a soft pile on the bed. The raw silk shimmered ever so slightly under the ceiling light. My shoulders shot up. I loved my dress.

After talking with Christy that morning about how much fun the dance would be, it was only natural to be excited, on crutches or not. She made me believe walking into the dance on Kyle's arm would make every girl there jealous.

I was so excited about the dance—till I glanced down at my ankle dressed in a thick ACE bandage. If I weren't on the stupid crutches, Kyle and Christy would have had to drag me off the dance floor at the end of the night.

I slipped into my dress with my makeup done to the best of my ability and my long blonde hair hanging with loose curls around the ends. Wearing one of the new shoes my mother had bought, I hopped over to the floor mirror.

My appearance shocked me. For the first time, I didn't resemble a kid. I could have been in any John

Hughes movie and fit right in. Move over Molly Ringwald.

Balancing myself on one heel, I spun around to get every angle. *Looking pretty darn good, if I do say so myself. What will Kyle think? If he wants to kiss, I better be ready this time. I can't look like an idiot tonight.* My mind raced a mile a minute, considering everything from how to give Kyle a real kiss to what to do when he touched me. All were things that I'd never done before.

"Tatum? Kyle just pulled up," Mom yelled from the top of the steps.

I had to make sure to walk slowly no matter how excited I got. Wiping out in such a short dress would not be good.

When I turned the corner of the living room, my mother had opened the front door for Kyle. He entered as if a spotlight shined on him. He was calm, cool, and collected.

He hadn't noticed me standing there.

"Mrs. Duncan, how are you?"

A star football player knew how to make an entrance, wearing a dark blue suit with a white shirt and slick black shoes. His hair was held back with gel that showed off his blond highlights from the sun. He looked great. Immediately, my heart fluttered.

I felt proud to be going with Kyle. I must have been delusional the previous week. Kyle had chosen me! My body shuddered from the first volt of a nervous chill.

"Oh, I'm fine, but look at Tate." Mom waved her hand at me from the doorway.

Kyle looked me right in the face, wearing a bright smile. He examined me from head to toe, stopping at my feet. His mouth dropped. "Tatum . . . what happened? Are you okay?" He hustled over to me.

Mother looked outside, then back at me. "The limo's here. Come on out and let me get pictures before you guys go." She hurried out the door with her camera in hand.

"Sure, it's just a sprain I got roller skating. I'm sorry, but I don't know how much dancing I can do."

"That's fine. I mean, why didn't you tell me?" Kyle kindly responded.

I held my breath. "If you knew, would you still have wanted to take me? This way you see I'm able to go. It's no biggie."

"You're right. We'll find other things to do. I'm just glad it's a sprain. You could have broken it."

Kyle moved his hands to my hips and tightened his grip. "I'm glad to see you're able to go, though. You look beautiful tonight."

"Thanks. You look nice yourself." I mumbled under my breath, "Real nice."

I stopped myself from examining him from head to toe.

Inching toward my face, Kyle never took his eyes off of me. I took a few quick breaths. His lips were just inches from mine. I said a quick Hail Mary, thanked my teddy, Mr. Bigalow, and closed my eyes

"Tatum, we're waiting to take pictures. Kenny, can you get Tatum out here?" Mother yelled from the lawn.

I popped open my eyes.

Kyle took a step back. "Your mom is right. Let me get you to the limo."

It wasn't so much what he said, but the look he gave me. His eyes narrowed and darkened. That moment I'd felt someone else in front of me. Not the cool, laid-back jock who had asked me to be his girlfriend days prior.

Christy and Eric joined us in front of the rented limousine for pictures. Between my mother and Christy's mother, it felt like we were in a New York model shoot. Typically I would have been annoyed by my mother demanding a ridiculous number of poses, but not this time. What I paid attention to was how Kyle stood behind me with his hands gently holding my waist. To my surprise, I rested my hands over his. His skin was soft. Warm. I glanced over my shoulder back at him. He tilted his head at me.

He reached down and gave my cheek a tender kiss. "You're beautiful, Tatum."

When he spoke, his breath brushed my neck. The tickle caused a shiver to zigzag down my spine. I considered that move brave in front of my parents, especially my father. He watched us with his ex-boxer arms crossed over his chest. Mother continued snapping away.

After a million photos around the limo, our mothers let us leave. Kyle thoughtfully helped me inside, then took my crutches and tucked them away. We all took a seat, Kyle next to me. The driver closed the door. I took a second to examine the interior. Blood-red velvet curtains hung from the small, curved windows. The seat upholstery was of the same lush velvet. I'd never seen inside a limo like that.

Kyle slipped his arm around my shoulders and snuggled up against me. I didn't need to read him to know he liked me. I liked him, too. Although I felt he had other plans for tonight than I had. This was my first high school dance. And I was going with the star football player everyone was talking about. Nothing was going to stop me from enjoying this.

The limo pulled up in front of the main doors. Immediately a small crowd stopped and looked at us. I took a deep breath—crowds were never my thing.

Christy put her face in the window between the red velvet curtains. "Ha . . . look at 'em staring at us." She sat back just as the limo was put in park. "Yup, we arrived in the coolest car, thanks to Tate. I mean, who shows up in an old Mob limo?"

A Mob car? When I'd first seen the limo that hadn't crossed my mind, but when Christy said that, it rang true.

Eric looked at Christy as if she had four heads. "How do you know what a Mob car looks like?" He chuckled, clearly amused by her car comparison.

She shot her nose upward. "My mom and Dad just watched *Bonnie and Clyde* on cable. I'm not a complete idiot, Eric."

She glanced at me with a twinkle in her eyes. "Have you ever seen the movie, Tate? Warren Beatty is a hottie."

The driver opened the back door. "Can I help you out, miss?" the driver asked, his hand out.

Kyle shot up before I could answer. "I don't think so, buddy. Here, you can take her crutches, though." He handed my crutches off to the driver, then jumped out. Kyle turned around and put his hands out to me. "Here, Tate. Come right here. I'll grab ya." He pointed to the doorway.

I did and was out of the limo in one single sweep. My body was now in Kyle's arms, and he gave me an excited smile.

He was holding me to him and examining my face. "Did I tell you how great you look?"

"Yes, you did." I giggled. Whatever I saw, or thought I saw, back at my house was gone—thank god.

"Well, I'm gonna tell you again."

But instead of telling me, he tucked his bottom lip in and bit down.

Ducking my head back an inch, I said, "Kyle, we should go inside. It's cold." The last thing I wanted was for other people to watch me during "the kiss."

The driver handed over the crutches. Kyle slid his hand around my backside, trying his best to help me walk. He stopped and turned back to the driver. "Excuse me, driver, before our time is up, we'd like to go get dinner. We should be out in a couple of hours. Thank you."

Unfortunately, not only were people staring at me on crutches, but the crowd was pointing at the limo, the old Mob limo. I was shocked my mother had chosen that car.

"Come on, Tate. Don't worry about the stares," Kyle said, giving me a little squeeze.

"Thanks." It was reassuring knowing Kyle would be at my side all night.

He ever so gently kissed the side of my cheek.

We four walked inside and took the table nearest to the door of the senior gymnasium.

In the middle of the gym lay a large wooden floor that students were dancing on. No one cared about the glittery hearts in red and silver dangling from the ceiling, but they took full advantage of the unusually dim lights. Red-and-white balloon bouquets were scattered around the room. A large disco ball reflected off the girls' dresses, making the decor appear more extravagant. The dance was exactly how I'd imagined it.

Curious to see how my dress rated among others, I sat down and surveyed the crowd. Eric and Christy ran off to the dance floor without even taking seats.

Kyle took my crutches and leaned them up against the wall. "You tired, Tate? You look out of breath."

"Yeah, maybe a bit. That was a long walk on those things."

He sat next to me, took my hand, and then patted the top. "You rest for a minute. I'll go get some drinks."

I looked at Kyle's face, examining his every feature—the softest blue eyes, thick lips, strong jaw, and perfect sandy blond hair kissed by the sun. My boyfriend was handsome.

Kyle cupped the side of my face. "I'm the luckiest guy here." He leaned in. His eyelids slowly drooped the closer he got to me.

Meeting him halfway, I was ready for my first real kiss. Not just a peck, "*the* kiss."

I sucked in a breath of air before our lips touched.

But my boyfriend went flying past me. I braced myself so Kyle didn't flip my chair over.

Behind Kyle stood the football jock who'd punched him on his shoulder. Not only was the jock laughing like a hyena, he'd ruined my first real kiss.

"Go get a room," the jock teased.

Kyle turned around and gave the guy an equally hard punch.

Acting casual had somehow fooled me into forgetting there would've been dozens of people witnessing my first kiss with Kyle. What I needed was Tom Cruise's aviator sunglasses to hide behind.

Kyle stood up. "I'm going to get us drinks, Tate. What do you want? Soda? Wait, you like tea, right?"

All embarrassment vanished. He remembered. I placed my hand over my heart. I'd never had a guy recall my drink preference. "Yes, tea would be great. Thanks."

He shot me his pointer finger real fast. "You got it."

While Kyle was gone, I noticed the dance floor was packed. From time to time, I caught myself swaying in the chair to the music. My ankle might have been screwed up, but my hips and shoulders were working.

Moments later, I spotted Kyle coming back, holding two drinks. Then another group of football players stopped him. It didn't take long before they had my boyfriend laughing and messing around.

Minutes went by before Kyle returned to our table. He placed the half-empty cups down. "Sorry, Tate. I spilled some of it."

"That's okay. Thanks for getting them." After taking my cup, I looked up at Kyle and smiled, but he had already put his back to me and was talking to his friends.

He had football friends come and go for the next hour. It was lonely sitting there, talking to no one but my half-spilled cup of tea. Not that I wanted Christy to sit with me all night, but watching her laughing and dancing with Eric made me jealous.

"Um, Kyle," I said, "don't mean to interrupt you. . ."

Kyle spun around, walked up to our table, and leaned down to me. He placed his hands on the table and locked his elbows. "No prob. What's up?"

The way he looked at me made me reconsider worrying about the audience for a kiss. Pathetic how badly I wanted any attention at the moment. "I was thinking. I really don't need this ankle to dance. With some help, I won't even need the crutches. Can we dance?"

He leaned down to my ear. "I know something else we can do, and you definitely won't need that ankle or those crutches."

I bit my tongue. I wanted to kiss him, but nothing more. That *was* what he was implying, right? His teammates were eavesdropping. This was a delicate situation.

I cleared my throat. "Um, thanks. But maybe later."

His lips rubbed alongside my ear. "That's okay." He backed up to face me. "You're right. There's a lot of people here. We can leave soon." He gave me a quick kiss on the lips and walked back over to their huddle, leaving me to sit there.

I wasn't sure what to think. I'd asked him to take me dancing. Then he'd suggested we do something else. Or maybe he didn't want to dance because he couldn't.

No matter how I tried to rationalize his reaction, I decided it was time to walk around. I grabbed my crutches.

Kyle interrupted one of his friends and turned to me. "Where are you hobbling off to?"

"I'm going to go to the bathroom. I need to stretch for a minute. I'll be back."

"Sure. Be ready to go in a while. We need limo time."

There he went again with the limo bit. Kyle and his beefhead friends watched me hobble off. I wouldn't look at them, but I couldn't help seeing that they began to whisper in my boyfriend's ear.

"Hey, where are you going?" Christy's voice came from behind.

"Just walking," I replied.

We walked for a while before Zach Bertano headed toward us. He always took my breath away. Wearing black slacks tailored to him and a shiny black button-down shirt with the cuffs folded up, Zach resembled an Italian male model walking the runway. Poised and confident. Even with his hands in his pockets, he was perfectly balanced. Talk about stunning.

It became incredibly hot in the school all of a sudden.

Christy leaned over to me. "Jesus. Zach looks awesome. Nobody in this school dresses like that."

He acted as if he were moving in for a hug, but apparently he decided not to.

"Tate, what happened?" He eyed me up and down, stopping at my chest area.

It was a challenge to walk on crutches without "the girls" popping out. After my face caught his attention again, I explained about the fall and then changed the subject.

"Who did you come with, Zach?"

"A group of friends. We're getting together back at my house after the dance. Would you like to come? Christy, you're welcome to come, too."

Christy and I looked at each other in awe before I turned back to him.

"Um, thanks, Zach. But we're here with Eric and Kyle. My parents actually got us a limo, so we need to go home with the guys. Thanks anyway."

Christy jerked her head toward the dance floor, "It's 'Purple Rain.' Where's Eric?" She looked around for her boyfriend, then bolted.

Zach and I stood there watching her drag Eric out to the dance floor. Couples slowly swayed side to side in each other's arms in the soft light.

I was losing out again. My heart wished Kyle and I were swaying in each other's arms. I looked over to where my boyfriend stood. He was still there, laughing and carrying on with some other football players. I read him loud and clear.

Suddenly, a hand graced my arm.

"Tate, would you like to dance?" Zach asked.

"Um . . . not sure. I came with Kyle. Besides, my ankle."

Zach glanced to our table on the other side of the gym. He saw the same thing I had. My date would not be asking me to dance, now or ever.

He turned back to me. "I'm a friend. And friends can dance. Here, I'll help you."

Zach led the way to the opposite side of the dance floor, near a hall that led to the locker rooms. He escorted me just around the corner and rested my back against the wall.

"Here." He took my crutches from me.

From out of nowhere, his blond friend, Tyler, showed up and took the crutches. Tyler stood off to the side holding them while staring at everyone else—bizarre demeanor.

Suddenly, my heart went into overdrive. Zach Bertano was pulling me into his arms.

He held me upright by taking my waist. Then his warm hand interlocked with mine and he swayed us to the music. "Did Kyle at least tell you how beautiful you look tonight? 'Cause if he didn't . . . I'll have a talk with him."

A nervous giggle escaped my lips. "He did, Zach. No worries."

"You look great, but you always do. How's the ankle holding up?""Uh . . . it's okay. Thanks."

After noticing how we fit in each other's arms, I relaxed. There was a new feeling inside me, one I'd never actually felt before. Zach and I had known each other for years, but we'd never touched like this. There were a few guys I'd dreamt about dancing with, but none of them were as handsome or exciting as Zach.

His other hand pressed against my back, sending chills from my head down to my toes. If that wasn't enough, he walked that hand up to my neck and caressed my nape, sending a light, pulsating tingle up my spine. He continuously moved his hand to touch different parts of my back side. I exhaled, moving my shoulders toward him to cuddle, loving how good his hands felt on my skin. Soft. Warm. Gentle. He embraced me. Our bodies couldn't get any closer. His chest was expanding the same way mine was. Slowly, I trailed my gaze up to his. He swallowed, taking a deep breath as our eyes met.

He had gorgeous eyes. Intense. Strong. Jet black. I liked that. And he smelled like sandalwood. I really, really liked that.

With his eyes locked on mine, Zach stopped swaying. He released my body and slid his hands to the sides of my cheeks, cupping them. His eyelids drooped. I slid my hands to his waist.

The moment our lips touched, all was forgotten . . . my surroundings . . . the pain from my grandmother's death . . . Kyle.

Zach made me feel invincible, and I never wanted to leave his arms.

The tingle and desire I felt were forbidden, though—wrong time, wrong place, wrong guy.

Coming to my senses, I took a step back from him, from his lips, and dropped my hands from his waist.

I stared at his lips, the lips that had given me my first real kiss. The best kiss I'd ever had. In that moment, I knew I'd never be the same again.

The music was fading to its end.

Tyler coughed and moved toward us.

My knees felt weak. I reached out for my crutches before I collapsed to the floor.

Tyler coughed again, louder this time. "You're cutting it close."

He's right. What was I thinking? Dear lord, I pray no one noticed us.

Zach straightened and stepped back.

I quickly tucked the crutches beneath my arms as Tyler headed toward the walkway.

Not knowing what to say, I stared at Zach's shiny black shoes. "Thanks for the dance."

His hand brushed my shoulder. I looked up at him. It was clear that he wanted to say something, but he didn't. I wanted to ask what he was thinking, but I knew I had already crossed the line. Kyle was my boyfriend, *not* Zach.

Zach shouldn't have been my first kiss. "I gotta go."

He nodded. "I understand. Take it easy going back to the table. Everything'll be okay."

How could everything be okay? If anyone told Kyle, he'd break up with me. Not to mention the reputation I'd get. And I felt different . . . way different. Damn it.

"Yeah, sure." I looked back, and Zach was gone. Just like that, he'd disappeared.

Navigating around fellow students who were walking off the dance floor was tricky enough, but when Christy grabbed my arm, she made me jump.

"There you are. Kyle's looking for you."

"Thanks. How was the dance with Eric?"

She smiled as if she'd convinced her parents to hand over the new car for a whole weekend. "Slow and sweet. Just the way I like it."

"Oh." I was shocked by her implication. Was I the only one at the dance who didn't have their hormones raging?

On our way back to the table, I looked around for Zach. How could he have taken off so fast? That's when I spotted Tyler, leaning against the side wall, watching Christy and me.

I had a feeling someone else was watching, too. But who? Or it could have simply been my conscience saying what a lousy cheater I'd turned out to be.

I refocused my attention elsewhere, and there he was. Zach.

Never taking his eyes off me, he walked parallel to us, along the rim of the dance floor. He gave me the same cozy, warm feeling I got when lying in my heated waterbed underneath soft flannel blankets. With a slight grin on his face, he had his chin slightly tilted down and eyes piercing through me. Then he nodded. Just a simple nod. Nothing more.

Something told me we weren't just friends.

Something turned on inside me.

Something made me want to run up to him and kiss those lips until the sun came up.

Dang it . . . I'd joined the hormone party.

"Look, Tate. I gotta tell you something before we get back to the table," Christy said.

Uh-oh . . . busted! I came to an immediate halt.

She looked right at me. "Um, Kyle's been drinking," she hesitantly said.

Drinking? Oh. That I could handle. "His friends probably gave it to him."

We continued on. A few moments later we were back at the table.

"There you are. You ready for dinner, Tate?" Kyle asked.

He seemed more than chipper.

"Sure. Let's get the driver."

In the backseat of the limo on our way to the Olive Garden, I could smell booze on Kyle's breath. My guilty conscience was killing me. Did he drink because I wasn't at the table? Because I was off dancing . . . kissing Zach? Maybe if I had been with my boyfriend the whole time he wouldn't have been drank.

The hostess sat the four of us in a quiet corner. Kyle cozied up next to me, and his hand went straight for my knee. Eric sat on my other side.

The waiter introduced himself, and my attention stayed on the menu, plus Kyle's hand. He had strong fingertips. I couldn't help but compare Kyle's touch to Zach's. I remembered the tingle Zach had sent shooting up my spine, as if a wind funnel spun around us, holding me in place. The most magical thing I'd ever felt.

"Tatum? Hello. Tea?" Kyle tapped my wrist.

"Oh, yeah. Tea." I grinned up at the waiter. "Yes, tea would be great. Thanks."

I had to stop thinking about Zach's kiss.

We were all having a great time, but the longer we sat there, the quieter Kyle got.

A while later, the waiter delivered our dinners.

"Manicotti, miss." He slid the plate in front of me.

It smelled great. I smiled up at him. "Yes, perfect."

The waiter turned to his tray, grabbing another plate. Meanwhile, Kyle tilted his head at me with a stony expression.

The waiter placed Kyle's plate down next, then the others', before asking if we needed anything else. Eric told him no, and the server walked away.

"Would you mind not drooling at the waiter in front of me?" Kyle blurted out.

I looked at Christy and Eric to see how they were going to respond to Kyle's weird comment, but they were looking at me with raised eyebrows.

I turned to Kyle. "Oh . . . are you talking to me?"

"Who else would I be talking to? I saw how you two looked at each other."

"Kyle, I have no clue what you're talking about."

"Don't lie. I saw how you made eye contact with him. 'Yes, perfect.' And pull the top of your dress up. You give him one more peek and I'll—"

"Calm down. I was saying the food was perfect. Not him." I pulled my dress up and glanced around to see if anyone overheard us arguing. We were clear. "Kyle, you got it all wrong. I'm really enjoying this. Please." I reached over and touched his shoulder. "Thanks for taking me out. This really is nice."

He exhaled and grinned. "You're welcome."

Kyle leaned toward me and kissed me without warning.

The smell of booze startled me, but I didn't dare move away from him. I had to give "the kiss" a solid chance. Even if we were in a restaurant, I had to give more to this kiss than I had to Zach's. A moment later it was over.

Kyle leaned back, grinning.

I looked at him.

He watched me, waiting.

The kiss . . . nothing. I felt absolutely nothing. I tried—

"How's the food tasting? Everything okay?" I heard the waiter's voice.

Kyle froze, his face turning red. Then he slowly backed up from me and rolled his head to the waiter.

Eric stirred in his seat. "Everything is fine. Check back later, please."

I made sure to keep my head down, eyes on the food. Even though Kyle had gotten the wrong impression and kept giving our waiter dirty looks, it was a nice meal. So when Kyle threw down just enough money to cover the bill, I was shocked.

"If that prick thinks he's getting a penny for staring at my girlfriend all night, he's got another thing coming."

Nobody said a word. The service was good. There was no reason to stiff the waiter.

Eric had his wallet out and seemed to be counting to himself. It wasn't fair for Eric to cover our tip, assuming that's what he was doing. Kyle folded his wallet and tucked it away.

Keeping my clutch under the table on my lap, I slipped out a ten dollar bill. This would be the best magic trick I'd ever performed. Folding the bill till it became a tiny square, I tucked the square between my fingers and closed my hand.

I kicked Eric's shoe under the table and loudly exhaled. Then with the bill hidden in my hand, I reached back and pretended to yawn, stretching out. As my arms came down, just underneath the table, I flicked the bill onto Eric's lap. Kyle only noticed the top of my dress creeping downward. I gave my boyfriend a bright smile.

Taking a glance at Eric, he grinned, shaking his head. Eric tucked all of the money in the black folder and placed it on the table. "It's set. Are we ready to go?"

Outside, in front of the restaurant, the driver held the limo door open.

Kyle jumped in first, then put his arms out. "Come here, Tate." One swift lift and I was in Kyle's lap. "Now, where were we?"

CHAPTER 5

Somehow, I escaped the dance with my reputation intact. Kyle didn't find out about me and Zach dancing. Or kissing. Nor did he find out about me tipping our waiter. Both things could have ended my relationship with him. And although Kyle had fast hands, I really liked him and his company.

That Friday, at the end of lunch, Andi and I decided to walk outside the school to avoid the crowd. Once we made it to the other end of the building, she opened the metal door for me. Not paying attention, I carelessly hit the door with my crutch, causing Andi to lose her grip. The door came at me, catching the top of my bandaged foot.

An extreme, intense sting vibrated from my toe up to my head. And in the moment, I was sure the whole school heard me scream like Steven Tyler.

I hopped around on the good foot.

"Tatum, oh my god. What did I do?"

"Andi, get me to the nurse's station. Quick." Something bad must have happened to my toe; the pain was unspeakable. The really bad news was that we were at the opposite end of the building from the nurse's station. This would be an agonizing trip.

"Oh crap, seriously? I can't carry you."

"Please, my toe. Oh god, it feels broken."

Tears started rolling down my face as she put my arm around her shoulder. We hobbled up half of the flight of steps.

"Don't look down," Andi instructed.

I looked down.

Blood was soaking through my sock. Footsteps were rushing toward us.

"Tatum, my god." Zach gasped.

Before I could ask for help, he scooped me up in his arms. Andi grabbed my crutches and followed.

"What did you do this time?" Zach's face showed concern.

"Why is this happening to me? Since my grandma died—"

"Don't cry, Tate," Zach softly said.

Andi was right next to me. "Jesus. You're dripping blood all over."

Taking a quick glance behind Zach, I saw there was a trail of blood spots. "Zach, put me down. I don't want to get blood on you."

He remained focused on carrying me. "No, I'm not putting you down till we get there."

Zach had come in and taken control, no questions asked, and he most definitely didn't hesitate. My eyes wandered to his face. He was serious. Then just as quickly, he glanced straight into my eyes, our eyes met. We stared at each other without a word. *The kiss.* Our kiss flew to the forefront of my mind.

Zach flashed that brilliant smile at me. His eyes lowered at the same time he rolled his bottom lip in before slowly rolling it back out. I had to stop staring at his lips, so I closed my eyes and tucked my head on his chest. For a moment. He rested his cheek on the top of my head. I was comfortable. The feelings my body was experiencing in his arms were a good distraction from the pain in my toe. Wrong or right, Kyle and I didn't have this connection and flare between us, not like Zach and I did.

Zach was taking me all the way through the high school to the nurse's station, farther than the length of a football field. He seemed to be my knight in shining armor. I kept my face in his shirt when I noticed people coming out of their classes to watch the horror scene going down the hall.

My arms squeezed around his neck a little tighter. If he dropped me, that would only lead to more injuries and embarrassment. We finally turned the corner to the office, and Andi ran ahead to get the door.

The office staff ran out of their cubicles in order to help guide Zach to the nurse's office in the far back corner. We stormed into her office and Zach gently sat me on the first bed.

"Oh dear, what happened?" Mrs. Thomas, the nurse, dropped everything and came running over. She thanked Zach and told him he could leave. He reluctantly walked out, continuously looking back at me.

The nurse slowly took off the bloodied sock. I bit down on my knuckle. Andi held my other hand.

"How did this happen?" Mrs. Thomas asked us.

I hadn't looked yet, but I could feel a cool breeze and stinging on what felt like a skinned, raw toe.

Andi told her what happened, and Mrs. Thomas replied, "Tatum, your nail is popped up off the nail bed. We're going to fold it back down."

When I looked at my foot I felt nausea. "*Aaaaaahh, Jesus Christ.* My nail . . . *shit!*"

༺ ༻

An hour later, and after a lot of pain, Andi and I went to our last class. She carried my books for me. I had to be very careful not to put my toe down. It was a good workout for my right leg. Andi put my books down on a desk while I gave the biology teacher the hall pass. My foot was absolutely huge with all the new additional bandages. No sock would fit over my foot. Andi gave me a hug and left, whispering that she would call me later.

My biology teacher said, "Tatum, let me know if you need anything, hon."

"Yes, ma'am, thank you." I took a seat.

"Tate, are you okay?"

I glanced over. I hadn't realized Zach was next to me. "Yeah, I am now. Thanks for earlier. You saved me, big time."

That's the first time I noticed something in his dark, black eyes. The look in his eyes made it clear he cared about my well-being, and so did the way he'd insisted on carrying me across campus. Would Kyle have jumped in and reacted like Zach did? Unfortunately, I didn't think so, unless he thought I'd make out with him for gratitude. But it didn't matter if Kyle would have or not. Zach wasn't my boyfriend and I should not have liked the way I felt in his arms.

"Tate, are you okay? Is something else bothering you?"

People always told me my face showed everything I felt. This would be one of those times.

I couldn't look at him. "Oh, yeah. I'm just a little upset about something. Thanks, but just forget about it."

"Sure you don't want to talk? I'm all ears."

A boy "all ears"? Boys hate talking. I glanced over at him. He seemed sincere, though. But I seriously doubted he wanted to rehash our kiss. "Um, no thanks, Zach, but that's really nice of you." I turned back to my studies when the teacher walked up to the chalkboard.

The bell rang, announcing our last period had come to an end. I was gathering my things when Zach offered to carry my books to the bus.

"Thanks, that'd be great."

"No problem. I wanna make sure you don't hurt anything else on the way to the bus." He smirked at me.

"Ha-ha, funny. Tomorrow I'm actually shooting for breaking the leg entirely."

We made it to the bus, and Zach walked me on and waited for me to take a seat. He handed me the books once I got situated.

"Be careful. And good luck at the doctor." Zach stood there, staring right through me.

Anxiety vibrated through my body from my head down to my toes, so I looked away, because I couldn't face another uncomfortable moment of staring at his lips. "Thanks. I'll need it," I said to the window.

Zach didn't walk away. He continued to stand there. I had to give my knight a proper thanks, no matter how awkward, so I decided to face him. But as I opened my mouth, Christy walked onto the bus.

"Hey, I heard what happened to you today."

Zach and I ignored her for the moment and grinned at each other. Then just like that, he turned and walked away.

Christy took her seat. "So, I heard—" Christy paused until Zach was completely gone. "So, anyway, I heard Zach carried you across the school to the office."

"Uh, yeah. So? It was a good thing he was there. He's a lifesaver."

"You know Zach's in my fifth hour, right?" Christy asked me.

"No, I didn't know that."

"Well, anyway, he was talking about it, and I got the impression that he likes you."

He likes me? Dear lord. If that got out . . . our kiss . . . "He does not. He was probably shocked by what a mess I am and felt sorry for the idiot, me."

"Oh, stop it, but seriously, you could tell."

"Wait a minute. Weren't you the one . . . oh, I don't know, a few weeks ago . . . telling me that Kyle liked me and that I should go out with him? Chris, please do me a favor and find yourself another charity case—"

"Tate."

I pointed at her. "Not another word."

For once, Christy obliged. I stared out the window the rest of the way home.

What's going on with me? I feel like since I've been with Kyle, I've been a total mess. I almost failed my biology test. I've made stupid mistakes and experienced bogus accidents. And every time I've tried to read Kyle, I've been way off. And Zach only complicates things further.

That night, after we got home from the doctor's appointment, I made calls to my girlfriends and then to Kyle. I had to let them know no activities, bed rest till Monday. Besides, the doctor had given me a small supply of Tylenol with codeine for the pain. That alone would knock me out.

The doctor's orders were a blessing in disguise as far as I was concerned. Taking the weekend off would give me a chance to refocus my thoughts and attention on my boyfriend.

Nothing could ever happen between Zach and me. Ever.

CHAPTER 6

February 27, 1989

Monday morning, I got off the bus and went to find Zach. He was crouched down, riffling through his locker.

I hobbled as quickly as I could to get to Zach's locker before Kyle saw me. Zach spotted me and stood. His face brightened with a gentle smile. The kind of smile I'd imagine a Groom would give his beautiful Bride the moment he saw her walking down the aisle toward him. I could get used to that smile. He was my knight in shining . . . but no, that had to stop. He wasn't my . . . anything, especially not my boyfriend.

I stepped up to him. "Morning, Zach."

"How did it go with the doctor? I was tempted to call you." Zach, being a gentlemen, grabbed my book bag for me.

Immediately, every sensation that Zach always awakened zinged through my body. Damn it.

I closed my eyes for a moment to collect my thoughts before responding to him. "Yeah, about that . . . actually, I wanted to thank you."

"Thank me? For what?"

"My doctor made it very clear that if it wasn't for you getting me to the nurse so quickly, I might have lost the nail. Did you know if you lose a toenail it could screw with your balance and the way you walk?" I sounded stupid. Ever since the dance, I'd been nervous about talking to him.

Zach chuckled. "Oh well, then thank god yours was saved. Could you imagine the accidents you would have without the nail?"

Ignoring any cuteness, I said, "Yeah . . . anyhow, thanks again, Zach. You really did save me."

"You're welcome." His hand went to the side of my arm. "I'm just glad you're okay."

His touch—definitely zinging. I took a deep breath.

"Thanks. I'll see ya later." The moment I took a step back, Zach's eyes hardened. Something behind me had caught his attention. Before I could see what he was looking at . . .

"I've got my girlfriend's bag."

I turned to look behind me. "Kyle. Hi. You startled me."

"Let's go. Now," Kyle demanded, nodding his head for me to walk away.

Zach gave Kyle the look of death and said, "What—is—your—fucking—problem, Jock Boy?"

A strong gut feeling told me to get Kyle out of there. Or maybe it was what Zach said to him. I put a hand on Kyle's big chest. An altercation in the hall at school was the last thing any of us needed. The principal would not let it go this time. "There's no problem. Kyle, let's go," I insisted.

Kyle glared at Zach—face red and nostrils flaring like a bull ready to take on the matador—and jerked his new football jersey back in place.

"Thanks again, Zach. See ya later." I had to get Kyle out of there.

Zach nodded, but didn't take his eyes off of my boyfriend, daring him to make a move.

Over at my locker, I turned on Kyle. "You completely embarrassed me."

"Look, Tate. Sorry, I just don't like how he acts like he's always there to save the day. Zach Bertano . . . to the rescue of a beautiful woman," Kyle continued to huff.

Christy, Eric, and Andi stayed back—a reluctant audience to what had just happened. Smart move.

I flung books, folders, and my jacket in the locker. "You know what? I was thanking him for reacting so quickly Friday. My doctor said because of Zach, I still have my toenail. So yeah, he did kind of save the day. Sorry." I slammed my locker shut and readjusted my weight on the crutches. "Just forget it."

"You're right." Kyle physically spun me around to face him. "I get it. I'm sorry. How 'bout this weekend I take you out. Movies and then dinner? Just the two of us, on me?"

I let out a big breath. "Fine, if you want to."

He pulled me into him and squeezed. "You smell so good. I love your hair, Tate. Look, I'm not mad. You're in my arms."

Fighting with Kyle wasn't my intention. I looked up at him. He looked down at me.

"This was a good thing. Your girlfriend's nail was saved," I said.

"Maybe I should go personally thank him. You do have sexy toes," Kyle snickered.

A month later, Kyle dropped me off after another evening out.

There was never much point in sneaking in the door after being out all evening, but that didn't stop me. But the moment the door latched . . .

"Tatum?"

I spun around. "Mom?"

"Did Kyle drop you off?" "Yeah, he already left." Why did she insist on bothering me after I got dropped off? Who else would have driven me home when I was out with Kyle?

She followed me up the steps into the kitchen. "He's bringing you home too late."

"You said eleven." I glanced over the stovetop. The digital clock flashed ten fifty-five. "I'm early."

"You left your clothes in the dryer. You can't go out unless all of your chores are done."

Exactly why I'd wanted to sneak inside. She was fishing for a screw-up by me. "Fine." I walked toward the hallway, hurrying to my bedroom, hoping to avoid a fight.

"How's it going with him?"

I stopped and turned my head over my shoulder. "Peachy. Thanks." I continued down the hall. *Wait. Mom's reaching out like Grandma said she would. This is a first.*

Changing my mind, I turned back. "Actually."

Mom stood in the kitchen, adjusting her weight. "Yeah?" "Things have been going good. Except for one thing—"

"What is it? Did you do something?"

And just like that . . . the hope for a change in our relationship was only a fantasy. She would always assume I was the problem with anything that went wrong.

I scratched my head. "Nah. Actually, never mind. Everything is going well. Goodnight, Mom." I went to my room.

If Grandma were still around, there wouldn't have been any words to induce guilt or any indication of wrongdoing. She would have authentically cared how things were going. Like how much of a gentleman Kyle was: showing me off to his parents, taking me to the mall, the movies and restaurants, taking an interest in my hobbies. For the past month, I'd had a great time with *my* boyfriend. That is, most of the time, but for one thing.

Kyle had random mood swings.

CHAPTER 7

April 1989

Kyle and I didn't have the perfect relationship, but what couple does? Certainly not my parents. The only thing that mattered to me was that we had fun, and things were bound to get better. Although I could have done without Christy walking around, gloating, "I told you so."

Till . . .

We were on the school bus heading home. The weekend had officially started, and Christy asked if I would go to the mall with her, just us girls.

"Sure, I'll go. Sounds like fun. We haven't gone with just the two of us in months."

We headed down the street to our houses. Christy had been quiet for a few minutes. She wouldn't look at me. There was that look of *I know something you don't, and you're not gonna like it*.

"I was thinking . . . I already talked to Eric about going. Maybe you should talk to Kyle," Christy said.

"Talk to him about what? I don't need his permission. But I'll let him know I'm going."

Christy shrugged, "Okay."

Walking past the mailbox, I grabbed the mail and headed inside. I dumped my stuff on the dining room table, got a handful of Fig Newtons, then sat down on the bar stool, flipping through the mail.

Bills. Bills. Credit card offer. Death certificate.

There in my hands was an envelope from Missouri Vital Records. This had to be Grandma's death certificate. My chest hurt.

There was Grandma and me together. The trip we took to New York just four months ago flashed in my mind.

Grandma and me laughing at each other while lying in bed, telling stories . . .

Grandma showing her playful side by playing tricks on my uncle every night . . .

Grandma hugging me at Ellis Island, saying how much she loved me . . .

The memory of her hurt too much. As if getting stuff out of her house hadn't been enough, now this was shoved in my face. I was trying to move on, but the constant reminder of what I'd lost kept punching me harder than Muhammad Ali.

Deep in thought, I hardly noticed Gizmo was barking in the backyard until there was a sudden banging on the front door.

I sprinted to the front door, shouting, "I'm coming. I'm coming." I used the back of my hand to wipe tears away.

The moment the dead bolt clicked, the door flew open. I jumped back so the bottom of the door wouldn't catch my toes.

Kyle was standing there. "We need to talk about tomorrow." He stepped inside.

I shut the door behind him. "Okay."

"Whose idea was it to go to the mall without us guys?"

I examined Kyle's posture. Tense. *Read him, Tate. You need to try and read him. Patience . . . focus. Do it.* "It was Christy's. Is there a problem? What's wrong, are you going to miss carrying my bags?" I laughed—a piss-poor attempt at easing some tension.

Kyle wasn't laughing, though. "Why do you girls want to be alone? What . . . do you wanna scope for guys?"

"Um, no, we never said we had to go without you. She thought it would be nice for a change, just the two of us." That came off wrong.

"*'Nice for a change.'* What, are you tired of me already?"

I took a step back. He was mad about this: eyebrows furrowed, nostrils flaring, lips tucked in tight—the angry, jealous bull was back. Anybody could see that, but there was something else. It wasn't just being mad, he looked different. In the seven weeks we had been dating, I had never been scared of Kyle. Until now.

"I didn't say that. Why don't you do something with the guys? Don't you miss going out with the team?"

"Are you trying to break up with me? Is that it, Tatum?"

Suddenly, Kyle spun around, running his hands through his hair. With that movement his hand knocked a picture frame off the side table. I leaped, stopping it from hitting the floor. The saved picture was of my grandparents' last anniversary dinner with us. I took another step back from him.

"Why don't you like me?" He spun around to face me. "Is this why it's been hard for me to even get a kiss from you lately?"

No, it was because Kyle's kisses never felt like Zach's. That was my secret, though.

His chest pumped slower and slower. Was he calming down? That's not what I thought he'd do. He looked around and then ducked his head. Kyle grabbed me and tucked me up against his chest.

He placed his head on mine. What the hell was happening?

"I'm sorry, Tate. Look . . . you're right. You can go without me. I trust you." He stepped back and held my elbows. He looked down at me, trying to meet my eyes. "Babe, I said it's okay. Are you all right?"

Breathing again, I turned my head up to his. "I never said I had to go without you. You're overreacting again."

"I know. I do trust you, sorry."

Nodding at him, I said, "Sure. Just forget it."

He pulled me into his arms again. He gently touched me, massaging the back of my head, playing with my hair, telling me how sorry he was. Confrontation averted.

I put the picture frame back, then flipped on the TV. I sat next to Kyle on the couch and leaned into him. He went back to playing with my hair. The gesture made me relax.

"Kyle, I was thinking. Would you like to come over before I go to the mall tomorrow?"

That made it clear I was still going without him.

"Yeah, I think I will. Thanks."

The clock struck four fifteen. I heard my parents' van pull into the driveway.

Turning to Kyle, I said, "Well, that's my parents."

Kyle got up from the couch and headed for the front door. "I'll call you in the morning before I come over."

My parents came in the side door while Kyle and I walked out the front. "Dad, the mail's on the kitchen counter," I called out and then shut the door behind us.

I walked him out to his car.

Kyle got in the car and rolled down the window. "When you get inside, look in your purse. I put a note in there for you."

"A note? You've never written me a note before."

"Who says I can't? Just read it, you'll see."

Maybe it's a love note!

Once inside the house, I headed to the kitchen for my purse. My mom stood at the dining room table, a paper in her hands, reading. My purse sat wide open.

I slowed. Could Mom be reading my note from Kyle? I wondered if Dad took the Death Certificate. Yup. The stack of mail was gone.

Mom held the paper up. "What is this garbage, Tatum?"

Garbage . . . what was she talking about?

Since I wasn't answering fast enough, she repeated herself. "I said, what is this?" She snapped the paper toward me.

"What is what? That paper? I—"

"Don't play dumb with me, young lady. I found this in your purse, so what is it? I'm waiting, Tatum, and I'm losing my patience."

I was tongue-tied. My mom never really had much patience to begin with, and the paper didn't look familiar.

Since she was holding the paper out, I took a glance. It was noticeable there wasn't much written. One word stood out, though: *sex*. You could see that word from a mile away. My head was spinning. Would Kyle write me a sex note?

She snapped the paper again. "*Tatum?*" "Mom, I don't know. Kyle said he put a note in my purse, but I haven't read it yet."

"Tatum, this is nothing but filth. You tell me right now what you've done with this boy."

"Nothing, Mom. We barely kiss. I swear," I pleaded. How could I say, *I swear we only kiss . . . and I don't even like that*?

She shook the paper twice. "If I ever see anything like this in my house again, you'll be sorry," she snapped out at me. "And you tell your perverted boyfriend he best keep his hands off of you. Do you hear me?"

"Yes, Mom." I had never been so embarrassed.

She stormed past me over to the trash can. "I just don't know what I'm going to do with you. You're letting that boy lead you down a bad path, Tatum. Over my dead body, though." She ripped the paper to shreds. "As a matter of fact, you tell Mr. Kyle that he is *not* welcome back in my house ever again. Understood?" "Yes, Mom." I couldn't look at her rage-filled eyes. Maryville was in the distance.

She stomped over to the sink and grabbed the Brillo pad. After a few pumps of Lysol, she scoured the sink as if it were sheet metal. "There's no need for trash like this—at least not in my house. And to think . . . I thought you had a nice boyfriend. Boy, was I wrong."

Why did Kyle write the word *sex*? And my mom

had seen it. Dear lord. If there was one thing that set her off, it was sexuality. I couldn't even count how many times she'd told us that if she could do it all over again, she would have been a nun.

Dad emerged from the basement. "What in the world is going on up here? I can hear you screaming all the way downstairs. What's wrong?" Dad's eyes were red.

He stood on the top step, watching my mom scrub the sparkling sink.

"Nothing, Kenny. Just Tatum at it again. But I got it."

Dad looked at me. "You okay, Tate?"

That broke my heart. I knew Dad had been down there reading his mother's death certificate and there he stood, asking me if I was okay.

"Yeah, Dad. I'm fi—"

Mom jerked around. "What? Of course she's okay."

Dad nodded at me and walked away.

I looked back over at the table, and there lay my purse, wide open. It amazed me that she'd seen my purse and decided to go rooting.

I gathered my belongings and went to my bedroom, wishing I had done so to begin with. Moments later, I heard Mom talking to a neighbor outside. I called Kyle.

"What in god's name was in that note you wrote me?" I yelled.

"What? Why? Didn't you read it like I told you to?"

"Well, I was going to, but when I came in the house, my mom was reading it."

"Oh, no."

"Oh, yes, and boy, is she pissed at you. What did you say besides the word sex?"

"I thought you said you didn't read it?"

"I didn't. She held it out, and that's all I could spot. You wrote it in caps, you idiot."

"Shit. Never mind."

"Are you kidding me? After I just got chewed out, and for what? I can't believe you're not even going to tell me everything it said. This is bullshit, Kyle. My mom's coming back inside. I gotta go."

Something in my head popped. Life at the moment seemed too much to handle. I blurted, "And I'm glad you're not going to the mall with me tomorrow. I could use a break." I slammed the phone down on the receiver.

If nothing else, I had control over that.

The next morning, my family had already left for grocery shopping when I rolled out of bed. I slumped to the kitchen for a bowl of cereal, sat at the table, and watched the microscopic TV my mom had on the counter. The phone rang, startling me.

"Hello?"

"Tate, it's Christy, can we come over?"

Choking on my Lucky Charms, I managed to get out, "*'We'*? Who's 'we'?" I looked down at my pajamas.

"Me and Eric. We'll be right there."

The phone went dead.

Jumping off the bar stool, I headed for the front door.

Just when I reached the knob, Christy and Eric barged in. I jerked back out of the way, feeling déjà vu.

They hustled inside.

"What's wrong with you guys?"

Christy shut the door behind me and locked it.

"Okay . . . you guys are starting to scare me. What's going on?"

Eric didn't take his eyes off of me. "Kyle's on his way over here."

"For what?" That reminded me. "Hey, do either of you know about this letter—"

"*Yes*," they said in unison.

"Great. Finally, someone can tell me what it said—"

"No," Eric said curtly, "Look, Kyle's really pissed off at how you talked to him on the phone. Hanging up on him wasn't a good idea, Tate. Now he thinks you and Christy are going to the mall to pick up guys."

I studied their faces for bits of humor. This had to be a joke.

Christy looked as if the Grim was standing in front of her. Oscar for her if this was a joke. Eric, best supporting actor.

"This is so stupid. Why would we try to pick up guys when we have boyfriends? Besides, let him come over so I can find out what he wrote in that stupid letter that got *me*," I pointed at my chest, "screamed at by my mom last night."

I dropped onto the couch, putting a pillow over myself.

Gizmo barked like crazy in the backyard.

Then the same banging as yesterday started on the front door. Must be Kyle's signature.

Christy ran for the seat next to me.

"Come in!" I sang.

Eric walked over to the door. "Hey, man, what's going on?"

Kyle pushed past him. "What are you doing here?"

"He's here with me," Christy chirped.

"It doesn't matter. I wanna know what that letter said, Kyle," I said.

"Why did you hang up on me last night?" Kyle was fixated on me.

"Jeez. Why is it so hard to tell me what you said? And you have the nerve to come in here demanding to know why I hung up on you? I almost got grounded because of you." And little did any of them know what we'd received in the mail—that didn't help my mood.

"Anyway, my mom doesn't want you over here. Ever. Do you know she asked me what we were doing? Like if we've done it." Their jaws dropped. "Yeah, now try that one on for size."

Kyle's face softened ever so slightly. "No, I didn't know your mom asked that." He looked at me. "I thought she liked me. Never, though?"

"No, never again. Not after that note." I took a breath. "Look, I know I said that we could hang out today, but that's not going to happen, considering you're banned from my house. I need you to go." I started to casually shove off from the couch when I heard some kind of growl. Thinking Gizmo was inside, I looked up, but he wasn't there.

Kyle yelled, "That's it? You just shove me to the side? I've done nothing but treat you like a goddamn princess, and this is the thanks I get? 'Get out of my house'?"

"Okay, you can leave now. You're missing the point." I said, heading to the door.

"The hell I am. I wanna know why you hung up on me and why you don't want to be with me. That's the fucking point, Tatum."

"I never said I didn't want to be with you." Although I surely didn't want to be with him then. "It's my mom and this stupid note. You don't know how she gets once she starts yelling."

Kyle took a step closer to me. "You don't hang up on me. Got it?"

"Okay, fine. But you still need to go. If my parents catch you here—"

"You tell me to leave one more time, Tatum, and you'll be sorry. Now tell me why you don't want to see me toda—"

Eric placed his hand on Kyle's shoulder. "Dude, you need to calm down."

That was a mistake.

Kyle flung himself around, knocking Eric's hand off of him. "Get your fucking hands off of me."

Then Kyle shoved Eric.

"What the hell?" was all I could say.

Christy and I backed up, fearing the swinging fists.

Eric didn't let that go. He went after Kyle full speed ahead, shoving him into the wall. When Kyle's head thudded against the wall, they both froze. Kyle looked over at me. He was still pinned to the wall by Eric.

I couldn't look at him. Just another confrontation with my boyfriend, although it had never escalated to that point before. This roller coaster with Kyle was not what I'd had in mind when he asked me to go steady. *This can't be what it's like. This can't be as good as it gets for me.*

Kyle threw his hands up. "All right. I got it, I got

it. Tate?" Kyle's voice was soft.

I looked up at him. "Yeah?"

Eric relaxed.

"I'm sorry. I should go. Have fun at the mall. I'll call ya tonight after you get back."

Kyle walked out, not looking at anyone.

Christy and Eric turned around together and stared at me.

I was in shock. "What the hell just happened?"

※ ※ ※

At noon the next day, I sat there, still not knowing what to do or think about me and Kyle. He'd never called me like he'd said he would.

Someone was at my front door.

I checked the peephole. Kyle stood there with his head dropped. In that moment, I felt mentally exhausted.

"What?" I called out through the seam. I watched through the peephole.

Kyle turned his head up at the door. "Tate, I'm sorry. Can you let me in so the neighbors don't hear?"

"No. I don't wanna argue."

"Please open up. Look, I want to apologize. Please?" Opening the door could be the biggest mistake of my life. Or it could mean Kyle did care about me and wanted to work on his temper.

I made him wait. If he would be patient, then maybe he was sorry. I still watched him through the peephole. Kyle looked around the neighborhood a couple of times. Then he leaned up against the door. "I know you're watching me, babe. I wish you'd let me in so I can apologize right."

He had been patient. I took one last breath and unlocked the door. He stepped in and embraced me, squeezing me tight, then tighter.

"I'm so sorry, babe. I don't know why I did that. Please forgive me. I know I'm a jerk, and you don't deserve that."

Dear lord. From a psychotic rage to a mushy, pouty puppy dog, he was more hormonal than I. "First, you know you shouldn't be here 'cause of my mom. Secondly, sorry won't cut it anymore. You overreact too much."

"I know. That's why I got you something. You were looking at this when I took you to the mall last week. Hope you like it."

He reached in his letterman jacket and pulled out a bottle of Poison perfume. A big bottle. No one had bought me a gift like that, especially a boy. "Oh, wow, Kyle." Then it hit me like a sack of potatoes, all good feeling gone. "Thanks, but buying forgiveness won't work either."

He handed it to me. "I know it won't, but I really am sorry. I don't know how else to convince you. It's just my stupid mom running away, or I mean moving away."

"Running away? What do you mean?"

He stepped away and ran his hands through his hair. Kyle's nervous pace began. "Mom was glad Dad never touched me, but he wouldn't stop using her as the constant scapegoat." He turned again to face me. "Suppose divorcing him wasn't enough. Now she bought a house in Ohio. She's moving when school's out."

Just when you think you have problems, someone else has to top your shit. In my family, it was my mom who was the asshole, not my dad. And if my dad left me, I would be crushed. I couldn't even think like that. No wonder Kyle had mood swings.

"Do you wanna talk about it?" I sat down on the couch. "I'm sorry, but why isn't your Mom taking you, then?"

"'Cause Dad doesn't treat me like he does her. And I don't want to move away."

That made sense to me. I wouldn't want to transfer schools either—we were halfway through. And Kyle was the star football player; you don't walk away from that. Terrible to realize a parent was leaving you behind. How would I feel if I were in his shoes? Crappy. Moody.

I popped off the lid and sprayed the perfume. It was heaven, even though it was called Poison.

Kyle stood before me with a grin. "It smells good on you."

"Thanks."

"You know I care about you. When I saw your face yesterday and how sad you looked, it struck me. I never wanna hurt you. Am I forgiven?"

I took a deep breath. "Of course. And I'm sorry, too."

Kyle pulled me up to his chest again. This time he bent his head down along my neck and gently kissed all the way up to the top of my head. He was soft and gentle. He reached my forehead and kissed it. "God, I love your long hair." He examined my hair while running his hands down the front length. "I'll see you at school tomorrow. And you better be wearing that perfume."

He walked out.

I felt things between us were much better, that

there was a mutual understanding between us. We both had screwed-up parents. But Kyle and I could move past them. Together.

CHAPTER 8

Things became even more awkward in my house between my mom and me. My mom didn't even want Kyle calling when she was home. I swore she stayed home many nights just to make sure he didn't call.

Then to add insult to injury, she insisted I spend all of my weekends helping them set up my grandparents' house. The family was putting it up for sale. It just kept getting better.

When we were working on Grandma's house, I would escape to her sunroom. Back when she was alive, we'd sit out there and talk until our mouths went dry. I sat on the floor where her couch used to be and pretended we were talking, hoping to feel some connection. But I was always alone.

After my grandparents' house went up for sale, my parents seemed to relax a bit.

I spent very little of my free time with Kyle—Mom was not forgiving him just yet. I only prayed we could get over this hump. My mom was ruining any progress Kyle and I had made. Maybe I should've broken up with him. But things had been great between us, and I wished for that again. It was nice.

The last week of school, Kyle reminded me that he was going to Ohio for summer break. His mother needed help moving and getting settled in.

I was glad he was going out of town. Not because I wanted to be away from him—the opposite was true. But with Kyle out of town, maybe things between my mom and me would settle down.

Once Kyle left town, Christy threw a surprise sixteenth birthday party for me at my house—she invited Andi, Diane, and Val. Val went to a neighboring high school, but we'd met when we were kids. Our parents had lived in the same apartment complex when they'd first gotten married.

No new car for me, but that was all right. I missed doing girly things. I missed doing anything with my girlfriends.

Since I had started dating Kyle, most of my girlfriends had been put on the back burner, with the exception of Christy. It was nice to know Mom was in on the surprise and told all the girls they could spend the night. Like I'd imagined, she was delighted that Kyle was gone for two months.

My family went out for a few hours, leaving the house to me and my girlfriends.

Being alone gave us the opportunity to jump in the pool, simple things like that that my mother didn't allow because someone could get hurt. Once the sun went down, we stuffed our faces with great Italian pasta and salad that my parents had bought us earlier. I was having a great birthday slumber party. Simple. No drama. Easygoing.

Val was helping me clean up the dining room table where we'd eaten. "So, what shall we do next?" I asked.

"Let's play with your grandma's Ouija board," Christy replied.

I jerked my head at her. "What? That's not a good idea at all."

"Why not? It'll be fun. Right, Andi?" Christy nudged her. Andi shrugged. "I guess." Val stood next to me at the sink and whispered, "We don't have to, Tate, if it's too much right now."

"No, it's okay. I'll go get it out." Diane helped Val put the rest of the food up while I went to get the board. My father had it downstairs on his utility shelf, which was odd to me. The moment I picked it up I got a *bad* feeling. In the dim basement, I carefully examined the box. The box alone was creepy looking. *Oh, dear lord . . . please don't let us get spooked.*

We were all in my dining room. Candles were lit to make sure we were being completely stupid—Christy insisted on setting the mood.

Christy, Andi and I worked the board, Val dimmed the lights, and Diane sat watching, since she was afraid to touch it. Andi sat across from me, and Christy was on my left.

Christy and Andi were asking the board questions, moving the dial on their own. I followed them.

"Tell me what boy has a secret crush on me," Christy asked.

Andi snickered. "Yeah, tell me who's going to be my first boyfriend. 'Cause damn it, I know someone has to like me."

We all giggled.

I cracked open my eyes. Christy and Andi both had their eyes closed and fingers on the dial. It jerked away. Val and Diane were frozen in time.

"Tatum, stop jerking it," Christy laughed.

The dial went still, pointing at me. Christy and Andi popped their eyes open. Val flipped the lights on. You could hear Diane swallow from across the table.

"What happened?" Andi asked.

Di narrowed her eyes. "It fricking mo—"

I didn't think before speaking. "Nothing, Andi. We try again, and this time only I'm touching it."

Di shook her head at me.

The three of us tried again. We closed our eyes and barely touched the edge of the dial. I took a deep breath and whispered, "Are you real?"

I felt it moving and considered whether it was me. Pulling back gently, I slowly opened my eyes. It was moving by itself and stopped on the "Yes." I yelled to Val, *"Hurry . . . lights."*

My hands weren't even near the board, and the dial had moved on its own. I looked at Andi and Christy. "We do this again and by god, you keep your hands away so I can see them."

Andi shook her head. "You're crazy if you think I'm touching that board again. I saw it moving on its own."

Diane was sitting next to Andi. "I told you guys not to mess with it. Those things are cursed. Or portals. Or something."

Christy laughed. "Oh, shut up, Di, they are not. Come on, Tate, let's do this again."

I nodded. "I'll ask the questions." I stared into her eyes. Chris nodded back, agreeing to my terms. I saw the fear in her, but she'd rather have her teeth pulled than admit she was afraid.

Val flipped off the lights. Andi watched from her

chair, now backed away from the table. Christy and I slowly started moving the dial.

I spoke softly, "So you're real . . . okay, then tell me something I don't know."

The dial moved. I cracked my eyes open, and Christy had her hands resting on the edge of the table, nowhere near the board's dial. It slithered and slithered around the board, not stopping.

Thankfully Christy had her eyes closed, because I couldn't believe what I was seeing, and if she saw, there would be screaming. Rolling my eyes up, I saw Andi and Di sitting there, afraid to move—jaws dropped and eyes enormous.

The dial came to a stop on the letter B. It moved again, and then stopped on the E. Then to a W.

Shit . . . it was spelling something out.

Chris cracked her eyes open, but froze, looking like a deer caught in the headlights.

It stopped on the A, R, and then finally stopped on the E.

"BEWARE?" I whispered the word.

CHAPTER 9

Labor Day weekend 1989

Saturday afternoon, Val and I walked out of Famous Barr with bags dangling on our arms, proud of our mallrat status. We were busy deciding which tops to swap between us. She appreciated my quirky style and envied how I could pull old fashion together with new fashion, not caring if I wore skirts with "outrageous tights" and fifties-type sweaters.

"Thanks for doing something with me before we go back to school. I just feel bad. I told Scott I didn't want to go to the mall with him, and here I am with you," Val chuckled.

"I'm sure he wouldn't care. But thanks for going out with me before Kyle gets back tonight. I don't think we'll get to see each other anyway, but I want to leave it open just in case he can do something." A moment later I spotted Val's boyfriend. "Uh, don't look now, but Scott's over there, and he just spotted you."

A guy I didn't recognize was with Scott. Scott headed in our direction after waving to us. Then he gestured for his friend to follow.

Scott gave Val a quick hug. "What happened to you not wanting to go to the mall?" he said, eyeing her with a playful smirk.

She laughed in response.

"It was terrible, Scott," I teased. "She came here kicking and screaming. She didn't want to come with me to the mall, but I made her. Sorry."

Scott's friend joined us. The guy owned one cool walk and then some. One hand in his pocket. The other hand running through his wavy hair, as if it wasn't already perfect. Eyebrows so intense you could see them a mile away—dark and striking. He reminded me of Zach, cool and hot at the same time. The closer he got, the more my airway tightened. He walked up and said hi to Val. Then he looked right at me.

Scott smiled and said, "Tatum, this is . . ."

Beautiful. Handsome. Absolutely intimidating.

My mouth opened, but nothing came out. My mind drew a blank. I was mesmerized by this dangerous bad boy with the ocean-blue eyes.

"Tate, say hi, for Christ's sake." Val elbowed me in the side.

Ignoring the jab to my side, I blinked and noticed the guy's hand held out. I reciprocated. "Sorry, I'm Tatum. Nice to meet you."

His hand was large and soft as silk. Chills went spiraling down my spine. Pulling away from our handshake, I couldn't ignore how my body reacted to his touch. I stared at the floor to avoid their faces.

My face felt hot. Surely my cheeks were redder than Tammy Faye Bakker's. That's when I noticed his shoes. He wore old scuffed black biker boots with his pant leg folded up with a small cuff. His jeans fit perfectly. And he wore the coolest leather jacket. He seemed older than the guys I knew—he had a five o'clock shadow.

Val and Scott were talking, but their voices were on mute.

My stomach did a two-step, dancing around. I swallowed hard. *Keep it under control, you idiot. Jesus.*

Val nudged me in the ribs again. "Tatum, Scott was talking to you."

"Sorry. What?" I gently wiped my forehead with the back of my hand.

"What did you buy?" Scott asked.

"Oh, just some tops that were on sale. Nothing, really." I needed to walk away. Soon.

Scott's friend and I made eye contact. He had the nicest smile. Beautiful lips. I realized who he looked like—a dark-haired James Dean.

I couldn't breathe. This was crazy. I couldn't even look at him without reacting. I had to stare at the floor again.

Don't even get any crazy ideas. If he's staring at you, it's because you're acting like a freak show. Not because he thinks you're cute. A gorgeous guy like that, interested in you? He's the definition of cool, and here you are, looking like a ten-year-old girl with her hair pulled in a high ponytail and wearing black combat boots with a miniskirt. Jesus, maybe you don't *know how to make fashions intermingle.*

"We gotta go. See ya later." Scott kissed Val goodbye. "See ya, Tatum." He waved.

Mr. Beautiful had his hand out to me again. "Nice to have met you, Tatum," he said with a British accent.

British? No way. Maybe I heard him wrong.

This time I eagerly shook his hand. Once our hands folded together, his mouth closed and the corners of his lips curled upward. He stared right through me.

"Um, might, nice . . . to met . . . I mean, meet you too." Jesus, I couldn't speak. Then what the frick was his name? That was embarrassing. I slipped my hand back.

The guys waved and walked in the opposite direction.

I looked at Val. "I have to go to the bathroom, like right now. Please?"

"Sure." Val flashed me a quick, teasing glance.

"Okay, so bathroom and then a drink. No, wait." I stopped in place. "I need a cold drink first. Ice cold." I closed my eyes, running it through my head, since it seemed a little fogged.

"Yeah. I think you need to get the red out of your cheeks. You are so smooth, Tatum, it amazes me."

"Shut it, Val. You have eyes." I looked at her. "You know damn straight that guy has it going on." I chuckled. "What's his name again? I didn't hear."

She slapped my back, laughing. "Right. Didn't hear. His name is Nigel. And yes, he's British, Miss I'm-Too-Afraid-to-Even-Say-Hi."

I looked at Val and laughed. She knew what I was thinking.

Nigel. I liked that name. It was different.

༄༄༄

Kyle didn't return to St. Louis until the next evening, but he invited me to grab dinner out the moment he got home.

After we ate, I asked him to take me home. School was starting, and I needed to get on a better schedule. At least, that's the lie I told him. The truth was that my mother wanted me home by nine because school was starting. She was back to using any excuse to keep us apart.

Kyle parked his car a couple of houses from mine, in the dark. He moved toward me in a hurry. I thought his open hand went up. I jerked back, unsure of his intentions.

"Happy sweet sixteen, Tate." Kyle cupped his hand behind my head and pulled me closer.

"Aww, you remembered?" "Just because I wasn't in town doesn't mean I forgot your birthday. Jeez. Give me some credit, Tate." Then he kissed me.

Better, not too wet. I backed up, gathering my things to get out of the car.

Kyle didn't move. I put my purse on my lap and noticed he was glaring at me.

"Is something wrong?" I asked.

He looked out the front window, then back at me, his forearm resting on the steering wheel. "How long have we've been dating?" "Um, let's see. You asked me—"

"Officially five months."

"Right. Five months." I couldn't believe it had been five months. Time flew by. But could you count the last two months he'd been in Ohio?

He shook his head. "Five long months and not once have you touched me. Why?" My mind went back to his note about sex. Could he be ready? I wasn't. I wanted to remain a virgin until marriage if possible. It was important to me. Anyhow, he couldn't honestly think we were going to do anything in front of my parents' house? No way.

"Tatum?"

"I've never touched anyone like that, Kyle." Honesty was the best policy.

You would have thought I'd told him the funniest joke. "Are you shitting me? How did I end up with the most prudish girl in school? My god." He flopped back against his door. A second later, Kyle rolled his head toward me. "Do not tell me you're still a virgin."

Okay, I won't, then. But why is he asking me as if it were something bad? I always thought guys preferred their girlfriends to be virgins.

"Oh my god. You're shitting me?" Kyle looked down at my legs in a miniskirt. "But you wear short skirts . . . and whatever."

"Sorry? The fact that I prefer skirts over jeans does not imply anything more than my preference in clothes." Was he serious?

Kyle shot his hands up. "Okay. Okay. Calm down. Sorry. I would just like to make out with my girlfriend of five months."

It hit me. He was right. We kissed and cuddled sometimes, but we never made out. Why? What was wrong with me? *Damn it.* I cared about him and wanted to give the relationship the solid chance I thought it had.

I leaned toward him.

He came at me, kissing my face. His arms became tentacles, tousling my hair. "God, I missed your hair." His kissing went to my shoulders. I let his advances go.

To my surprise, my mind tricked me, and Nigel popped in my head. He was standing in front of me wearing that sexy grin and tousled hair. Reaching out for my hand.

Nigel took my shoulders. Then he leaned over and started nibbling my jawline. Down my neck and then to the other side. I kissed the parts my lips could reach, following his lead. My breathing increased. He was tender, even when he squeezed my breasts. His breath came faster. I took my hands up to play with his askew black wavy hair.

"Oh, Nigel," I moaned.

Kyle jerked back. "What did you just call me?"

My eyes shot open. Oh, dear god . . . "What?"

"You called me Nigel. Who the fuck is Nigel?"

"I didn't say Nigel. I said *not now*. Like not in my neighborhood, not now." Yep, that sounded good. I was a complete idiot, imagining this Nigel guy I didn't even know while kissing my boyfriend.

"What the hell, Tate? I'm sick of this with you."

"What do you mean?" I gawked back at him.

"You were getting all into it. Then you turned into the Ice Queen. What gives?"

Keep your hand on the door handle. If he goes crazy, run. "Not in a car, Kyle. Please don't get upset. It's okay to take this slow."

"I'm sick of slow. Now come here and touch me like you were going to."

I gasped. "Ew. Are you serious?"

"Yeah."

"That's it. I'm not doing this here in the car, in my neighborhood. Never. These people know my parents." I leaned over and kissed him. Pulling back, I said, "Thanks for dinner. I'll see ya tomorrow." I got out and quickly took off on foot, heading home. Kyle started the car, and the tires squealed down the street.

Friday, September 9, 1989

Yay! I'd made it through my first week as a junior. Only thirty-five weeks to go—then I'd be a senior.

Kyle was busy with football practice the whole week, leaving us very little time together. The initial thrill of being the girlfriend of the star football player had definitely worn off, making me wonder if there was anything left for us. The thought was sad, but not unexpected.

That Friday, Andi and I were walking back from lunch to my locker. We turned a corner to go to our lockers. Kyle walked straight for us, but he wasn't alone. He was holding cheerleader Bonnie's hand.

My legs wouldn't move another inch.

Kyle stopped.

"What's going on?" I asked. Finding him holding another girl's hand gave me a drop-kick to my stomach. Things weren't great, but cheating on me?

He dropped her hand as fast as lightning. "Oh, nothing, I . . . um . . . was . . . just helping Bonnie out with her ah . . . breakup . . . from, uh . . . Zach."

"Zach who?" I looked over at her. "I don't recall you going out with any Zach, Bonnie. The only Zach I know is Zach Bertano, and he's never talked about you." Of course, no one knew I hadn't talked to Zach that whole summer, and god only knew who he dated. I hadn't even seen Zach until the first day of school that week. I briefly glanced at Kyle to see if he would say anything, but to my surprise, he didn't seem to care. "Guess I'm just a little confused."

"Um . . . well . . . uh." Bonnie turned to Kyle for help.

Just what I thought. The whole Zach thing was a lie. Idiots. At least try *to look innocent. How dare they make a fool out of me?*

I put my hand on my hip and said, "So, what is it, Kyle, because Bonnie here is starting to break a sweat? And she doesn't look so good when her cake-face starts running."

Andi just stood there with her hand over her mouth, shaking her head in disbelief.

"Tatum, leave her alone. It's my fault. I thought you would get mad if I stayed with her to talk and uh . . . help her . . . get through this," Kyle sputtered.

"Oh, well, how very nice of you to help her out in her time of need. I'm sure you did her a great service. And the next time you touch another girl, maybe—" Wait. Next time? I found him holding another girl's hand and I would stay with him? Not likely. I had it.

"Um, actually, can you follow me?" I waved Kyle over, away from our company's ears. He stepped over to the side with me.

He folded his arms over his chest, glaring down over me. "What? You gonna tell me stay away from her?"

I glanced away so I didn't laugh in his face. Looking back at him, I said, "No, you can have her. She's all yours. Now you're not cheating on me."

His nostrils flared. His hand curled into a fist and he backhanded the locker next to him. "What? You're not breaking up with me."

"Yeah, I am, actually. Look, I'm sorry. I thought we had something—"

He grabbed my shoulders and put me against the locker. "The hell you are."

Kyle had me pinned against him. I wasn't sure

what he wanted, but I didn't want him touching me ever again. I felt dirty.

I shoved him away. "Stay off of me."

His mouth snarled up, growling at me. His hands rolling into fists again caught my attention.

"Fine with me. It's fucking over. I have bigger and better fish to fry." He stormed back to Bonnie. He took her hand and spun her around, pulling her away. "Come on, hon, let's go."

Bonnie looked back at me with a smirk. "Oh, did you tell her?"

"Yeah, I dumped her." Kyle shouted as they turned the corner.

It felt as if he'd smacked me across the face.

He dumped me?

That dirty bastard. I turned and kicked the lockers. I couldn't even punch them. No wonder he took me for a fool. How long had they been making an idiot out of me?

I ran as fast as I could to my locker, my hands covering my face.

Andi came up behind me once I dropped my forehead against the locker. An anxiety attack at school would not be good. *Breathe. Just breathe.*

"Tate? Don't worry. It'll be okay."

I rolled my head at her. "Thanks, Andi." I stood up. "You know, just this past Sunday, he was trying to get down my pants. So eager to move our relationship to the next stage. Thank god I didn't let him touch me."

She pulled me into her arms. "Yeah. Just think, you would have a similar reputation to Bonnie's. God knows that's not cool. Skanky cheerleader."

I backed up and smiled. "Right. Who wants to

wear red fricking ribbons tied around their ponytail? He must prefer girls with personalities like wet noodles."

Andi laughed. "Yeah, and yours a dry noodle!"

She knew how to make me feel better. Stupid jokes were the best. She apologized for not coming up with something cleverer.

Although Andi did make me laugh, I couldn't focus during my next class.

Damn it. I was a fool. That's probably where he was after practice all week, with her.

I didn't say anything about it to anyone the rest of the day. In fifth hour, once I took a seat next to Zach, he didn't take his eyes off of me.

I took a deep breath and turned to him. "Got a question for ya, Zach."

His eyes expanded. "Sure."

"Have you ever gone out with Bonnie?"

He jerked away, making a sour face. "Bonnie? The cheerleader who wears those stupid ribbons in her hair?""The personality of a wet noddle, the one and only. Yes." Funny that he hated those fricking ribbons too.

He sat back. "Not even if she were the last girl on earth. Why?""Oh, no reason. Just curious is all."

The bell rang. I settled into my desk and got my notebook out.

"Tate? Are you okay?"

"I'm fine, Zach. Just peachy. Thanks, though." I didn't look at him. His caring eyes would pull at my heartstrings too much. I couldn't wait to get home and have a good cry.

Even though my first boyfriend was a disaster and I knew we weren't good together, it saddened me. We did have fun at first. And it helped that Kyle was good-looking. And I used to be excited around him. The first time he'd picked me up, for the Sweetheart Dance, I'd felt good. I *had* felt good about us being a couple. That was over, though. He'd shown his true colors.

CHAPTER 10

The next morning, I had the house to myself. I laid on the couch, reading my favorite magazine, *Teen Bop*. Music was on in the background, and my life felt back on track. Finally. My weekend was off to a great start. No boyfriend to fight with. No Mom to keep me away from the boyfriend. I could do whatever I wanted. The thought put me in a great mood.

Gizmo barked in the backyard. A second later, there was a knock on my front door. Maybe it was Christy. It wasn't unusual for her to pop in without a call.

I looked out the peephole. Crap. It was Kyle.

"Yeah?" I yelled, struggling up on my tiptoes to the peephole for a better look.

"I know we broke up, but I'd like to talk."

"Talk? About what? Nothing will change."

He rested his hand on the door, as if he was holding on. His head dropped down. "Fine, but I'd like to stay friends. Christy and Eric are friends even though she broke up with him." He stared down at the peephole."True. But I don't think we should hang out. There's just nothing to talk about, Kyle."

I went back up on my toes to eye him. *Thud. Thud.*

Thud. He beat his forehead on the door. Kyle didn't appear to be getting the message—I wasn't interested.

"Come on, Tate. I found your tapes, they were in my bedroom."

Tapes? Those tapes had been "lost" for months. He found them?

"Come on, whatchya afraid of? Liking me again? Open up."

Now he was annoying. Me liking him again? I must have "stupid" written across my face. I wasn't sure I had the strength to deal with him, but I wanted my tapes back. I flung the door open. Kyle almost fell forward, but he caught himself.

"The tapes?" I threw my hand out. He slapped them in my palm.

After examination, I determined they were indeed mine. "Thanks for bringing them over. See ya Monday."

I got the door shut halfway before Kyle shoved it wide open. I staggered backward. Kyle stepped inside.

"What are you doing? Get out of here." He slammed the door shut behind him. The deadbolt clicked.

One large step and he breathed in my face. I wasn't sure which scared me more. The menacing expression on his face, or the stench of beer vomit on his breath—which made my eyes burn.

"I'm not going anywhere, Tate-um."

"Yes, you are. You're leaving." I moved to the side with the intention of showing him to the door. But Kyle didn't let me move an inch. He kept a fingernail's distance between us.

"That's what you think," he said.

The look on his face scared the hell out of me. And his bloodshot eyes looked worse than pinkeye. My gut ached. He couldn't be trusted. How could I escape?

"Okay." I forced a grin. If he didn't see the fear in me, he might relax. "How about we watch a movie then? I just bought *E.T.* We can watch that."

It was working. Kyle's shoulders relaxed a bit. He took a step back from me. "Yeah, that sounds cool. We'll get comfy first."

If he thought we were getting "comfy," he needed a reality check. "Absolutely. Let me go get the movie. I'll be right back. Maybe you can turn the TV on, you know . . . get it going."

Kyle stepped back and grinned, looking less threatening. But more sexed-up.

"Okay. Be quick."

I made sure not to make any sudden movements. Slow, easy steps to make sure he didn't change his mind. I took one last look at him before turning the corner for my bedroom. Kyle stared intently at me while flipping the TV on. I felt like I was in the eye of a tornado, looking at the storm that threatened to make me mangled debris. I had to get to the phone and quick. The closest one was on my nightstand.

"Be right back, Kyle." I quickly ducked into my room and grabbed the phone receiver. Every time I pressed a dang number the stupid phone beeped. *Shhh. Hurry, Tatum. Hurry.* I quickly dialed my mom's parent's number, praying my mom and dad were there. I needed my dad, and now.

The phone rang once. Thank god they weren't on the other line. I could feel my heart racing like it was in the Kentucky Derby. I took a few deep breaths as the phone rang another time. *Pick up. Pick up.* My hairline was wet. The phone rang again. I brushed the hair away from my forehead. I could have thrown up, my stomach churned with sour milk.

I blew out a puff, trying not to faint. *Breathe.*
I looked up.
Kyle stood in the doorway.
The menacing look was back.
I was going to be dead.
I couldn't react fast enough.

He grabbed the phone out of my hand and slammed it down. "I thought you were getting the movie." Kyle shook his head. "I knew you couldn't be trusted."

I ran for the other side of my bed, for the windows. If only I could scream. *Help!*

He'd trapped me. In this room. Nowhere to go.

Kyle imitated a tiger going in for the kill. Slow. Stealthy. Calculated.

He grabbed my shoulders and shoved me onto my bed. I crab-walked backward to the other side of my bed. Survive. Survive. I had to keep myself going.

Kyle kneeled up on the waterbed, following me. "I told you I wasn't going anywhere."

"We can be friends if you want. Fine. It's fine. Honestly." I casually stepped off my bed by the nightstand. Once my feet hit the floor, I ran. Full speed to the living room, going for the door. My life depended on it.

Kyle caught me around the corner, though.

With a wad of my shirt in his hand, he shoved me to the floor. My nails dug into the carpet, clawing. I'd grind my fingertips off if it meant escaping him.

I tried to pull away, knowing if he got ahold of me,

I could kiss tomorrow goodbye.

"What are you doing? Stop it, Kyle. Stop."

He jerked my shirt to one side, flipping me over. "Did you really think that you could tease me this long and not give me something? You should've done this months ago. Now stop fighting me."

I smacked him in the face. "Get off of me, you idiot. You're not touching me and the hell if I'm touching you. You make me sick."

He struck my face in return. My head whipped to the side. Ouch.

I wouldn't let him see me cry, but my cheek stung worse than a bumblebee sting. He could smack me, punch me, whatever he could try to do to me, but I'd be damned if I let him take it further.

"I make you sick? You fucking bitch, you owe me. I put my time in. Gave you gifts. Nice fucking gifts. Listened to you whine about your grandma. So what? She died. Get over it."

"Get off of me, you idiot." His one-hundred-seventy-five-pound body was not budging. I tried to roll him off, but no. Panic surged through my body. He laughed. I was only a ragdoll to his strength. "Kyle, I need you to leave right now." Nothing was working. He didn't respond. I was in a complete panic. I was trapped, trapped like a caged animal with no way out. I started flinging my arms around, smacking him in his face. Anything to try to get free from him.

"Stop it, Kyle! I want you to get out," I yelled. Within seconds, his face was marked with red scratches. I hoped the burn from the scratches would distract him enough for me to find a way out from underneath him.

He balled his fist.

Oh, god, no . . . I jerked my hands up, begging him not to.

One swift punch to my stomach. That's all it took to cripple me.

The mixture of smells—his beer vomit—my sweat—my fear—sickened me.

I fought, but couldn't get him off of me.

He ripped my clothes and took what I was saving for the man I'd love.

I never knew how much Kyle hated me.

Minutes later, there was a loud bang. The back door flung open so hard it shook the wall.

I heard something running into the house. Didn't sound like my dad, but I prayed it was.

I turned my head to the side as Gizmo came barreling around the corner. Snarling and baring his teeth, he headed straight for Kyle's bare rump. My heart sped up a notch from hope.

Kyle jerked his head toward Gizmo and pulled back.

"Oww. You fucking mutt." Kyle cocked his fist.

He was zipping up his pants as fast as he could and kept yelling, "Bitch, get your fucking dog. Stop!"

Gizmo was snapping at Kyle, then hopping back. Snapping and hopping back and forth. Kyle tried his best to fight Gizmo off.

I stood up and put my clothes back in place. I grabbed the corner of the TV to steady myself. I finished covering my exposed, bloodied body, but I was having a hard time standing.

"Blood. I'm bleeding," I whimpered. My body swayed and I could feel the sweat running down my face. Perspiration covered my skin. My body shook, and I was having trouble controlling my limbs. I hiccupped from crying so hard. It was gone. My virginity was gone. Just like that.

Kyle jumped up as quickly as he could while avoiding Gizmo. I yelled with what was left in me, "Get out. Just get out and never come back here, you filthy bastard."

I ran to bathroom, staggering, leaving Gizmo to finish him off. When I made it to the bathroom, I slammed the door behind me and locked it.

I could hear the front door flinging open and then Gizmo furiously barking.

"Ow, you stupid dog, let me go," Kyle yelled.

Gizmo yelped. The front door slammed shut.

The sound of the door slam shot through me faster than an AK-47. My life was changed. My life sucked. I had been raped.

I collapsed to the floor.

The weight of what just happened came down on my chest harder than a trash compactor. I couldn't take the pressure. The loss. The anger. The violence. My body curled into a fetal position and I sobbed like never before. My body continued to shake.

How could he? He said I owed him. And the one thing I wanted to happen on my terms, my way, he ruined. That asshole took my virginity.

Kyle had violated me in the most unspeakable way. Not once in the months I'd dated him had I ever thought this was plausible. I'd even felt safe around him, until the end. He had a temper, but this? No. I might've thought he would smack me, but rape never crossed my mind. Not once. Until today.

How could I have missed the signs? Were there signs? The moment when I had the door open and he shoved his way inside was the turning point. At that point, I was petrified of him. And to think, I thought he liked me. What did I do to deserve this?

Thump. A solid head-butt vibrated the door, distracting me.

"Gizmo?" I asked.

He head-butted again. He was waiting for me.

I reached for the wall; above me was the light switch. I took a cleansing breath and crawled my hands up the wall for support. I made it to my knees, my body excessively shaking, and then I pulled myself up the rest of the way. My shaky hands flipped the switch, and then I reached for the doorknob and pulled.

Gizmo sat on the other side of the threshold. He looked up at me with the saddest eyes. You could see his eyebrows scrunched together.

"I hope you got him good, boy. Love you, Gizzie." My voice came out broken and gurgling. Tears began escaping my eyes. But I forged out of the bathroom with my savior at my side. Together, Gizmo and I went around the house, making sure all the doors were closed and locked.

There was no sign Kyle had ever been there. At least, the house showed no signs.

My skin continued to crawl from filth. I had to get *him* completely off of me.

Back in the bathroom, I slowly took off what was left of my shirt. I let it fall to the floor. I pulled my bloodied panties down and put them, along with my shirt, in the bottom of the trashcan, under everything else.

I turned the shower on and stepped under the cascading water.

I reached for the soap, but my hands shook violently, making it hard to grasp the soap. I scrubbed myself as if I were sanding rough edges of sheet metal till my skin burned. Something bright colored caught my attention as it rinsed down the drain. I glanced down. It was blood.

That was Kyle. He did that to me because he wanted sex. And he didn't give a shit how he got it.

The thought of him still on my body was unbearable. Getting his sweat and the feel of his skin off of mine was urgent. I made sure my cleansing technique would be sterile enough for surgeons.

I stared up at the showerhead and watched the single drops of warm water trickle over me. The droplets tapped my skin, comforting me, telling me it was okay. I'd be fine.

I dunked my face in the stream—screaming till I lost my breath.

My eyes were closed, but tears still flowed from them. Each droplet that caressed my skin made me feel like my grandmother was there, holding me. The water wrapped around my shoulders. I needed someone, and I sensed her there with me, squeezing me in her arms as I wept. That's when I let out the most horrific cry. "Uhhhhh," I yelled, "that bastard. He took it. He stole my virginity from me. I'm so stupid."

The presence of cold water told me it was time to get out.

After I dried off, I stood there examining myself in the mirror, still shaking.

The naked person staring back at me was repulsive.

I didn't see an innocent girl any more. I saw a

broken girl.

Me. Broken. Shattered. In millions of pieces.

I guess sex was all I was good for. I'd never be anything. Did I think I was anything special? Different from the next vagina that walked by? I was nothing. And I was stupid enough to think Kyle cared about me. No one cared about me.

I reached in the vanity for my mother's shears. The one thing Kyle loved about me was draped around my face and my shoulders. And the sight of my long blonde hair made me sick to my stomach. There was nothing about me that repulsed me more than the symbol of beauty in Kyle's eyes.

I grabbed a sizable chunk of hair on the side of my head.

Chop.

CHAPTER 11

If I didn't feel like my life was over when Grandma died, I did now.

Gizmo lay next to me in my bed, letting me cry all over him. "You tried to tell me, Grandma, but I ignored the signs. Now I get what 'BEWARE' meant, when it's too late."

Knock. Knock. Knock on the front door.

Jumping up too fast made my head spin. Gizmo leaped off the bed and casually ran to the door, not even barking.

My experience flashed before me. *"Did you really think that you could tease me this long and not give me something? You should've done this months ago. Just once, why don't you shut the fuck up and do what I want—"*

Still in my bed, I crawled over to the window. My hands trembled, pulling the curtain to the side. No familiar car, like Kyle's. Why take chances, though? I yelled, "I'm calling the police." Still in bed, I fumbled for my phone.

Knock. Knock. Knock on my window.

Gizmo barked. Damn it, I had no energy to even dial the police, let alone try to fight Kyle again. My body wouldn't stop shaking.

"Tatum, it's me . . . Val. Are ya home? I got my mom's car today. Come on . . . we're hitting the town!"

Adrenaline seared through me, and without thinking I leaped for the curtain and jerked it back. She waved and smiled from the other side of my window.

My guardian angel was on the other side of the window. Feeling the weight lift from my chest after being scared shitless caused me to break down in tears. It wasn't Kyle. Nothing to be scared of. My heart was beating so fast, my chest ached.

Val's face went from a bright smile to a frown.

"Let me in." She darted for the front door.

Bracing my legs to walk, I held onto the wall all the way to the front door. Gizmo's tail was wagging. I unlocked the door and she burst inside.

I collapsed into her arms, hysterically crying. Crying so hard, my words skipped. "When *he* came over today . . . I thought . . . he just wanted . . . to be friends . . ."

༄༄༄

Sitting on my bed, Val grabbed my hands, still looking at my face.

"Ow," I said, freeing my wrists from her hold.

Val gasped. "Oh my god, Tatum. Your wrists . . . they're all marked . . . and swollen." She looked up at me.

It was one thing to speak about what had happened, but another to let someone actually see how weak I was.

Val jumped off of the bed, growling, and kicked my wall. "Oh, my god. That dirty bastard. Is he actually stupid enough to think he can do something like that and get away with it? That's it, we're calling the police." She headed for my phone on the nightstand.

I jumped up. Shit, that hurt. Val changed her mind and went for me instead. "Oh god, Tatum. Are you okay?"

"We're not calling the police—"

"What? Why not? Look at you, you can barely stand. I know you're probably in shock, hell, I'm in shock, but honey, he raped you.""I said no. I don't want anyone to find out. This is embarrassing enough as it is, telling you. And besides, you know what my mother will do. She's already threatened me with Maryville once before. I don't even want to imagine what she'd say about this. No, I'll be in an all-girls home faster than you can say, 'police.'"

Val stared at the floor for a moment. She knew that was something my mom would do to me.

"Besides, my dad will go over there to kill him and his father. I don't want Dad in trouble." My poor father had been through too much recently to find out his daughter had been raped on top of it. Not to mention, my dad was a boxer before he got married. He wasn't afraid to get in anyone's face.

"Fine. So do you know why he did this? Did he say anything before he attacked you?"

As I replayed it again and again in my head, my body began shaking. I could feel my blood burning. Him pulling me, tugging me, Kyle kissing . . . I whimpered, "He said that I owed him. That I should have given him that a long time ago."

"Seriously? That asshole. I can't believe he's—" I had never seen Val that furious before. She acted crazy.

"Look, I need to ask you something kind of personal," I said.

"Sure, of course, what is it? Anything."

"Well, I was wondering . . . do you think I'm okay down there? You know, afterward, I had blood all over me. I don't want to have to go to the doctor if I can avoid it. That reminds me, I want you to promise you won't say anything to anyone," I said.

"Of course I won't. You have my word." She bear-hugged me.

"Thanks. I knew you would understand."

Straightening back up, she continued, "Now, on the blood issue. I'm sure you're okay. It's normal for there to be some blood the first time. I take it this was your first?"

I nodded. The thought of him stealing my virginity and throwing it over the bridge was driving me insane. That was being saved for the man of my dreams, the guy I'd marry.

"And now, did he come in you?"

I began choking. She was so forward. "No. I don't think so."

"When was your last period?"

"I should start this coming week. Great. I didn't even think about that." I knew I could never talk to my mom about this. Val helped me more than she knew.

"Well, I don't think there's much to worry about. You said he was interrupted pretty quickly by Gizmo. You should be fine anyway."

With everything else to worry about, I hadn't even thought about pregnancy. I could kill Kyle. I used the back of my hand to wipe my eyes. "What should I do about Monday, at school?" I coughed. "He's in a couple of my classes this semester, and I really can't stand the thought of having to face him. Of course, I have to ignore him, but it's going to be nearly impossible."

Val gently reached for my shoulder. "Well, if you don't want anyone to know, then I suggest not looking at him. Ignore him. Stay clear and avoid him at all cost. Don't talk to any of his friends. *Nothing.* Ignore him, no matter what. He no longer exists."

I started imagining how hard it would be to avoid him completely, when I realized Val wasn't finished with her advice.

"Then, we're going to set you up with a new and much improved boyfriend."

"Oh, no," I sighed, as I threw myself back on my bed. *Ouch. My back. The carpet burned it when he—* "That's the last fucking thing I want right now, another stupid boyfriend." I awkwardly sat up.

Val's eyes were sparkling with revenge. "Well, I'm not saying today, but in the near future, very near." I could see the gears turning in her head; she was already scheming. "What's wrong with your back?"

"Nothing. Look, I really don't need another boyfriend, and I honestly don't care about revenge. I appreciate you looking out for me, but I'm at Randall by myself. I don't have you or Scott or anybody, for that matter, to look out for me."

"Tatum, if that nut job lays one more hand on you, I'm sure Scott will have no problem taking care of him."

"That's just it . . . I don't need any more attention right now. Actually, it would be nice if everyone would just pretend that *I* didn't exist."

"Well, we can—"

"No, just let me finish. I really can't explain how I feel, or why I feel like I do, so let me fade into the shadows for a while." I couldn't tell her death seemed like a good option at the moment.

"I understand. We just need to focus on you, and support you right now, got it," she looked away.

"I need to get some Tylenol. My head is about to blow," I said, slowly standing up.

"Sure, then I'm getting you out of here. You're staying at my house tonight. You haven't stopped shaking since I got here. Go get Tylenol. I'm calling your parents to make sure it's fine for me to take you."

Later that night at Val's, for the first time in hours, I stopped shaking. It did help getting out of my house. Val was right about that. If only the visions would stay out of my head. Val did her best to help. She took me to the mall for what I called 'new accessories.' They were leather wristbands that covered some evidence from where he'd held my wrists together.

After the mall, back at her house, we were getting ready for bed when I tossed my hat off.

Val's eyes popped open. "Holy shit. What did you do to your hair?"

I whipped around, my hand flying up to my head, not remembering that I'd cut it at first. "Oh, yeah, I did this after he left. You remember how he loved my long hair?" I'd put the hat on before Val had arrived, in case my parents came home early. Dealing with my mother about my hair was the last thing I cared to worry about.

Val swallowed hard. "Jesus, you went all out,

though, Tate. What's your mom going to say?" She stepped up to me and ran her fingers along the right side of my head—that side was shaved to the skin. Then she played with the short layers on top.

"At this point I don't care. She'll blow. But for some reason, I feel as if I can take it. She yells and yells anyway, so what's the difference?"

Val stood there, looking about the way I felt. Shoulders slumped, mouth turned down, eyes droopy and sad-looking.

"I can't believe this." She raised her head to me. "Tatum, I'm sorry this happened. I can't imagine—"

For a change, I reached out and took her arms. "Don't. It's okay. Don't they say what doesn't kill ya will only make you stronger? Well, I should be as strong as Superwoman now." *Yep, keep telling yourself that, Tatum, because you know damn well it's an act.*

She huffed an exhale and shook her head. "I love you, Crazy."

We changed without another word till I went in my purse for a brush. That's when I saw the Tylenol with codeine left over from my toe injury.

Val saw what was in my hand. "Do you want to explain those?"

"Remember the doctor gave me these because my toenail popped up? I need to relax, and this will do the job." I popped the last two into my mouth and chased it with water.

"Fine. I assume we're going to bed now anyway?" she said.

"I am. Then I'll be out until morning. But before these kick in I want to say thanks for being here for me, Val. I appreciate it."

Val's mom made us waffles before her family headed off to church in the morning. That was the only time Val got out of going, was when I spent the night.

"Your mom makes the best waffles." I took another bite.

"Yeah, thanks."

After we put our plates in the sink, we headed up the stairs to get dressed.

"Tate, can I ask ya something?" She sounded hesitant.

"Sure, what is it?"

She closed her bedroom door. "Did Kyle punch you or something?"

"What? Why?" I didn't want her to know the details. It was embarrassing. And I surely did not want to hear that fucking name.

"Well, last night, I noticed some more bruises on your chest when you changed into your PJs. And it looks like you got burned on your back. I don't mean to pry . . ."

In her room, I froze where I stood. The visions were back. The pain and burning . . . the smack to my face . . . His punches to my stomach and chest . . . My back burning from being thrashed back and forth on the

carpet . . .

Hands were on my arms, gently holding me. "Tate, you don't have to tell me. I assume anything I saw is from him."

I flung my head against her shoulder. "Thanks. I don't think I want to talk about it. Not right now."

She held me until my sobbing stopped.

"Are you sure you don't want to tell anyone? Like your dad?"

I backed up to look in her eyes. "Val, you promised."

"And I still do. It's just . . . Tatum, it looks horrible. What if he did some serious damage to your chest or something? And how are you going to explain all of the bruises and burn-looking marks?"

Convincing Val that no one would notice would be harder than convincing myself, but I was confident I could hide this. Grabbing Val's hand, I calmly answered her. "First of all, who's going to see my chest and back, besides you? No one. There's no need to start telling everyone because of the marks. They'll be gone in a week or so anyway. It's not like he did anything that won't heal on its own."

Val's face narrowed. "You don't know that."

"I said I'm not going to the doctor or telling anyone, and I mean it."

Val jerked back from me. "You can't hide everything with wristbands, Tatum."

"Watch me."

CHAPTER 12

Monday morning, my parents left before I even woke up. Dealing with my mom about my shaved head would wait until after school.

I stepped out the front door to meet Christy, and the wind blew right through me. Fall was definitely here. There was one observation about short hair—colder on your neck.

"Morning, Chris," I said, walking over to her. I should expect a lot of wide eyes today.

"Holy crap . . . your hair. That's a good way to piss your boyfriend off."

Exactly. "Let's just pretend my hair is still long and move on. And I'm not talking about boyfriends or lack thereof. So, how was work?"

Christy curled her top lip up. I knew she wanted to stop staring at my hair, but couldn't.

She had recently gotten a part-time job. Right up her alley, working with lots of guys from the neighboring high school.

"Work was good. I might be going on a date next weekend with this guy, Ben. I can't wait. He's so cute—red hair and blue eyes. It would shock you how sweet he is."

Great, let her go on about that redhead. Maybe she'd continue to keep her focus everywhere but on me.

It worked. Christy barely knew I was there. She rambled on all the way to school.

My first concern was getting what few things Kyle had in my locker out.

The bus came to a stop in front of our school.

"I'll meet ya on the bus after school. See ya," she said, and she ran off in the other direction.

I stood on the sidewalk for a moment and looked up at the huge brick building before me. Three stories tall, no windows around the main entrance but for the large front doors . . . it was a brick cell. If only I could predict how my day was going to play out. What would he say when he saw me? Could I avoid crying? Shaking? What stunt would he try? Surely Kyle would do his best to ruin my reputation. Just please let me survive no matter what he tried to pull. *Damn it, stop the shaking already.* I shoved my hand in my pockets. "Time to get the show on the road—"

"Get what show on the road?"

That voice. Everything I had gone through for the past two days jumped on my chest and sat. Had to keep my emotions under control. Deep breaths. School was not the place to cry like a baby. Just don't look in his eyes.

"Hi, Zach. How are ya?"

He was standing next to me, and then, as if it were completely natural, he walked me inside.

"I'm cool, how about yourself? I see you got a haircut."

Just move on, ignore the hair comment. You have more pressing things to worry about. "Oh, not so good, but I'm hanging in there." Why did I say that to him?

"Well, it looks like you're doing okay. New hair, new accessories . . . you're starting this year off on a different foot." He looked at my bracelets out of the corner of his eye, "I guess you went to the mall again this weekend? Suppose there's no need to ask what you did."

"Yeah, you know us mall rats." If I didn't smile, I'd break down a hundred times a day. Or just lock myself in my bedroom at home and curl up on the floor in a fetal position.

He leaned toward me and whispered, "I like the bracelets and hair. Different is good."

"Thanks." His words went through me like made-to-order comfort. A light bulb went off in my head.

"So, um, Zach. Do you think you could do me a huge favor? It's not a big deal if you don't feel like it—"

"Sure, what is it?"

Wow, that was quick. I didn't even get to finish. "Can you walk with me to my locker and then to my first class? I'd just really appreciate not being alone. I'm sorry, it's a lot to ask."

"Sure, but is everything okay?" Zach had one eyebrow cocked.

Stop looking at him. "Well, I guess you could say that the football player and I broke up. It wasn't exactly a clean break, if you know what I mean. I just want to avoid a scene at my locker if I can. I don't mean to put you in the middle or anything—"

"You're not scared of him, now are you, little Tate?" he said, raising his eyebrows.

"What? Me? Scared of him? Ha, ha, ha . . . you're

funny. Why would I be scared of him?" I swallowed. Snapping my head at him, I said, "Why, do I look afraid?"

He gave me that suspicious look again. I needed to get ahold of myself.

He said, "Oh, I don't know, maybe because you seem on edge every time his name is mentioned. But don't worry, I'll stay with you until we get to class. Even if you are a little chicken shit."

I didn't care if he was teasing me or not, my knight was back. Our kiss. It had been a long time since I'd felt good being with a guy. Not a surprise that the minute Zach walked into the picture, I felt safe. Why, though?

We were just a few lockers away from mine when I glanced at him and whispered, "If you could stay really close now, that would be great."

Scanning the hall, I could tell he was grinning, stepping closer to me, his shoulder touching my body. If Zach only knew what happened to my insides when he was so near.

To my surprise, Kyle was nowhere around, or at least as far as I could tell without looking too obvious.

Andi was at her locker. "Oh, my god. Your hair."

So maybe spiking my hair crazy like Aimee Mann's from 'Til Tuesday wasn't the brightest idea I'd had. I didn't look at her. I wanted to hurry up and get out of there. "I know. My hair. But can we talk at lunch—we're eating together, right?"

"Sure, I'll see you then." Andi shot us a curious glare, then waved her hand just before she walked away. I knew my hair would be the first thing she asked about at lunch.

Zach stood protectively at my side, leaning against the locker next to mine. It was kind of cute the way he stood there watching over me.

I opened the locker door. "Thanks so much for doing this for me. I really appreciate it."

"No prob. I'm glad to help." He touched my chin. "And don't worry 'bout your hair. It's cool. You should be glad to be different. Only you could pull this off."

He touched me. And tenderly. *His touch. Those lips. Stop. Don't look at him, not now.* Turning from Zach and toward my locker, I noticed something on the inside of the door. It was a pair of my underwear. Right above it was a piece of paper that read "cunt" in heavy black marker. I gasped. "Oh, no."

I snatched my stolen underwear at the same moment Zach crumpled the paper in his hand, cursing Kyle.

How could he do this? I did nothing to him. My chest felt heavy again. Holding the wadded underwear in my hand, I tried to figure out how long Kyle had had them. And not to mention how embarrassing it was with Zach seeing this. Forget trying to get through the day, I wanted to make it to first hour without an altercation with Kyle.

"Tate, are you okay?"

When I looked up at him, I could feel tears quivering in my eyes. They began to collect, enough to disrupt my vision. I blinked.

Putting his books down on the floor, he gently wiped the lone tear away.

Zach leaned in and whispered, "Tate, it'll be okay. He's a jerk. No one deserves to be treated like this. No matter how bad a breakup is."

I couldn't look at him. He was being so nice, and I knew if I looked up again I wouldn't be able to hold back the sobbing. He didn't know the extent of my "bad breakup," and yet he was being so sympathetic. More sympathetic than my mom would be, even if she knew what had happened. "I should be the one pulling crap like this. Not the other way around." I sniffled, forcing any sign of tears away. I stuffed the underwear in my purse and grabbed my books. Then, Val's advice ran though my head. "You know what? I think I'm going to walk around here as if this didn't even happen. Just ignore him. Then maybe he'll leave me alone, if I act like I'm not bothered by him. Maybe?" I looked to Zach for reassurance.

He shoved the crumpled-up paper into his back pocket. "It sounds like a good plan to me. And if it's okay with you, I'd like to walk you to all of your classes today. Do you think Andi would mind if I joined you two for lunch?"

"Would you really do that for me?" Never in a million years did I imagine us in that situation.

"Just for you."

"Then, no, I don't care. It looks like we'll be adding a chair to our table."

After second hour, Zach rushed over to my classroom door and walked me to my locker.

"I know I'm asking a lot today, but could we head to the bathroom before class?" I asked when we left my locker.

"Sure."

I opened the bathroom door and just barely stepped in before I turned to Zach. "I'll be right out." Turning back around to go into the bathroom, I realized I accidently opened the door into someone. "Oh, sorry," I said.

I looked at the girl. It was Bonnie, and she was giving me a dirty look. I stepped past the cheerleader, hoping the door would crush her.

Sauntering to the stalls, I called back, "Sorry . . . in a hurry, Zach's waiting for me."

I heard Bonnie sigh heavily and what sounded like the door closing after her. It felt as if I were in the stall for an hour, hyperventilating. Bonnie and Kyle were the last two people I wanted to see today. At the sink, I braced my hands on the sides of the basin. I glanced up at the mirror, not seeing Tatum. This was a different person. Someone new I'd have to get used to. *If we're in this together, I suppose we need to understand each other. First step, learn how to breathe again.*

Walking out of the bathroom, I saw Zach waiting patiently against the wall. We headed down the hall to my third hour.

"Did you say anything to Bonnie by any chance?" Zach asked.

"Why? Did the rat say I did?" I looked up at him, but continued walking.

"No, she didn't, but when she noticed me standing there it was as if I were a ghost. I thought maybe something was said."

"Jeez, why would I be hostile to Bonnie? Although I have every right to be."

"Oh, um . . . I don't know why I thought that. It doesn't matter anymore."

Well, look at that. He couldn't even look me in the eye. Rumors—or in this case obviously the truth—that Kyle had cheated on me had spread around the school faster than wildfire. Wonderful.

My third hour's door was right next to me. I didn't know if Kyle was inside or not. My hands started to shake and sweat.

Zach took a quick peek inside for me. "There's no teacher yet, but Kyle's sitting in there with another guy, I think it's Aiden. Wow . . . it looks like a cat scratched him."

I wanted to look at the damage I'd done to him, but pulled my head back just in time.

"Tatum, do you know how he got those scratches?"

When I spoke, I stared at the ceiling. "I do. I did it . . . when we fought."

There was no reply.

"I told you . . . it was a bad breakup." I exhaled, tilting my head at Zach.

"Why would he fight a girl?"

My heart was racing; I had to focus on breathing. "I don't know, but please don't say anything about it, okay? No one else knows about this, and I want to keep it that way."

I waited in a spot where Kyle couldn't see me. I took a deep breath and exhaled again. "Now, you promise you'll rush over here right after class?" I didn't expect my voice to shake, but it did.

"Of course, Chicken. I told you, I'm doing this just for you."

"You're so sweet. Thanks."

I started to move, and when I was smack dab in the middle of the doorway, I heard Zach say, "It doesn't mean anything, it's just for show."

Just as I inclined my head to ask him what he was talking about, he kissed the left side of my face.

"Oh, Jesus, Zach." I held my breath.

Zach looked at me with sultry eyes and whispered, "I'll see you after class."

Crap, his eyes, caring. I was dumbfounded. I was so screwed.

Rubbing my shoulder gently, he shot Kyle a venomous glare before leaving for his class a few doors down.

I trudged into the room, thinking about how I would like my tombstone to look, and took a seat in front of the teacher's desk, on the far side of class. I looked up at the chalkboard. I liked marble. Maybe Italian gray marble would be nice . . . I wanted to hold my breath until the teacher got there. No, I had to be stronger than the old Tatum. What was taking the teacher so damn long, though?

"So, you already found a new boyfriend . . . huh . . . *slut*?" Kyle shouted across the room.

I stared back down at my desk and decided to double-check my homework—all the while trying to remember what Val had said. It was hard. My hand shook as I wrote. But I was breathing, just breathing fast.

"Did you hear me . . . you slut? I guess you're doing what you do best."

That did it. That pissed me off. Doing what I did best? What? Fighting not to be raped?

Just as I was about to run over and attack him, Eric jumped to my defense. "Why do you have to be such a jerk to Tate? I'm sick of seeing you treat her like shit."

Kyle's response was a big, fat nothing.

The girl closest to me mouthed, "I take it you guys broke up?"

I nodded. Turning back to my desktop, I mumbled, "How could you tell?"

Then, I couldn't believe it. Eric moved to the seat right behind me. I noticed more movement and glanced over at the door. Finally, our teacher traipsed in and hushed the class.

I didn't hear another word from Kyle the rest of the hour.

I might as well have stayed home, since I stared at the same page for the entire class. I had no clue what the teacher had told us to read for fifty-five minutes.

The bell rang and I took my time gathering my things, waiting for Zach.

Someone came to my side and stood. I instinctively moved away and ducked my head.

"Sorry. Didn't mean to come up on you, Tate. But I like the hair. It's totally you," Eric whispered.

I relaxed my shoulders and looked up at Eric. Hopefully no one noticed my overreaction.

He grinned at me. Then he rolled his eyes in Kyle's direction, "Sorry . . ."

There was no need to let the guy feel guilty. "No worries, just go on. See ya later."

He nodded and walked off with a slumped head. I took a deep breath and exhaled. If Kyle was still back there, I had to get out and quick. Reaching for my things—

Kyle brushed by me, grunting, "Slut."

"Excuse me, Kyle, what did you just say to Miss Duncan?" Mr. Connors asked.

This might not be too bad after all.

Kyle kept heading toward the door, but called back, "I didn't say anything, sir."

If there was a best-shit-eating-grin contest, Kyle

just won. He walked out the door with a devious grin toward me. We made eye contact. I dropped my head faster than a hot pancake. The amount of arrogance he had with such a clawed face was quite impressive. I found myself snickering.

"I didn't think so." Mr. Connors peered at me over his reading glasses. "Tatum, is everything okay?"

I popped my head up at him. "Sure . . . everything's fine. I think *he's* just PMSing."

He chuckled for a second, then cleared his throat. "I see. Well, you let me know if you need anything."

"Will do, thanks."

A tall shadow standing in the doorway caught my attention. Then he whispered, "Pssst—Tate, are you ready?"

I knew it was my private bodyguard. "Yeah, I'll be right there." Walking toward the door, I said, "See you tomorrow, Mr. Connors."

He nodded and then got up after me and followed. I thought his actions were weird until I realized Kyle stood across from the door.

"Kyle, don't you have another class to get to? Don't linger in the hallway—move along now," Mr. Connors said.

Zach grabbed my books and we headed away from Kyle, toward the cafeteria.

Bam.

Zach and I jerked our heads back toward the violent sound. Kyle pulled his fist back from a dented locker door. It reminded me of how hard he threw a punch. If my ex had the chance, he'd kill me.

Zach put his hand around me and gave a tug toward the cafeteria.

He paused, staring me straight in the eye. "He did something to you. I know he did. But believe me when I say that he will never lay a hand on you again."

My breathing increased, signaling I was losing control. Zach gave my side a gentle tug. Reassuring me I was safe. He appeared to be my godsend. All the feelings I had for him were confirmed. Zach was not going to treat me like Asshole Star Football Player did.

We stepped into the cafeteria and walked over to my usual table.

"I think I'm going to go get my food first. If you don't mind? That way you'll have a minute alone with Andi when she gets here."

"Sure. Thanks, Zach."

Zach started to pass by me, but paused.

He softly placed his hand on my waist and just held me for a second. We stared deep into each other's eyes. Those caring eyes were back. Serious, deep black eyes. He opened his mouth, then closed it without saying a word. What did he want to say? Instead, Zach relaxed his features and exhaled. He dropped his hand and walked off before Andi got to the table. I stood there like an idiot, not moving.

"Tate, was that Zach? Of course it was, who else dresses like that? So, is he going to eat with us or something?"

"I guess you can say that he's both eating with us, and something," I said, studying her reaction to what I'd said.

"You're not with Zach, are you? Isn't he a little quiet? And scary? Besides, isn't that a little fast?"

"I didn't say I'm 'with Zach.' We're just friends.

And he's *not* scary. Just because he's quiet to you doesn't mean anything."

In the few minutes it took Zach to get his lunch, I had just enough time to fill Andi in on what had happened in class.

Andi shook her head. "Wow, Kyle's a jerk. I've never seen him act like that toward you before. Well, with the exception that he was cheating on you with Bonnie."

It was only natural for me to look at her cock-eyed. "Anyhow, that's why Zach's kind of being my private bodyguard for the day."

"And maybe the next day and the next after that, if I'm wanted," Zach said, putting his food tray on the table and taking the chair next to me.

Andi looked at him. "Well, that's mighty nice of you to help Tate out like that."

Zach turned to me. With a twisted mouth and soft eyes, he scanned me from head to toe. "Thanks." He sat down and took a bite of his pizza.

"Zach, you have a talent for walking up behind me without my knowing it. That's the second time you've done that to me today."

Clearly hungry, he shoved another bite in his mouth. "Yeah, I guess I do, don't I?"

"Andi, let's go get something to eat."

Before we stepped into the doorway for the lunch line, we both took one last glance at Zach. He was leaning back in his chair, watching us. We quickly stepped in the food line and out of sight.

I looked down and felt the blood rush to my cheeks. How frickin' cute was that? He was watching me.

Andi sighed, "Oh my gosh, how weird was that?"

CHAPTER 13

After Zach and I left the cafeteria alone, he said, "She wasn't so bad."

"What does that mean?"

"Well, I thought she was going to give us a hard time."

"Oh, I see . . . well, after I filled her in on what took place in class and then the locker, she seemed to back off some."

"What happened? Did he do something to you in class?" he said in a stern voice.

Zach looked mad. I had to act as casual as possible. "No, no, he didn't do anything, it's what he said in class, I mean—"

Zach's whole body went rigid. "What—did—he—say—to—you?"

"It was nothing. Eric stuck up for me and he backed down. It worked out as good as I could've hoped."

We were at our fifth hour door. I stopped him before turning for the doorway. "Are you sure you want to do this? Asshole Football Player will definitely react to you being with me."

Zach looked around and said to me out of the corner of his mouth, "I welcome anything he thinks he can dish out."

That was the last thing I wanted to hear. I knew it wouldn't be Zach starting it, and no good would come of him being involved like that. This was my problem, not his.

"And why are you so sure he'll try to start something?" He looked at me, placing one hand on the wall next to my head. His posture shouted power.

Our eyes met. "Zach . . . he's always been jealous of you. From the very first day."

He cocked his head to the side with an intriguing smirk.

"Yeah, I found out when you carried me to the office, when my toenail was ripped off. Remember? He didn't like that you were there to save the day. And how he came up to us afterward, when I was thanking you?"

Zach inched closer to my body, casing me within his.

He was inches from my face. "Yeah. So he's jealous of me." Zach grinned. "Excellent!"

I hadn't noticed the cold sweats had begun till—

"Tate, stop. If he sees you nervous like this, it's only going to make him happier. Besides, I'm capable of handling Kyle."

Hearing his name so much forced a constant chill down my spine.

Maybe if Zach weren't standing so close to me I wouldn't be so nervous. "I just want him to leave me alone, and I know with you there he won't be able to control himself. Not to mention, I feel bad for dragging you into this." Another stupid decision of mine. Zach should not have been involved.

"You didn't drag me. I offered, remember? And

besides, I wanna do this."

"Well, I really appreciate it." I patted his shoulder, hoping he'd take a comfortable step back. "Okay, so the plan is to act as if he doesn't even exist."

He backed up. "Got it . . . I think." Zach rolled his eyes up and twisted his mouth, thinking.

"Zach."

"I'm kidding, I'm kidding, calm down. Kyle who?"

"Funny, real funny." I looked away. "Just stop saying his name, please."

We walked into class and I took a seat in the aisle closest to the door, on the opposite side of the room from Kyle. Zach sat next to me, sitting so close I couldn't help but gawk at how tall he had gotten over the summer.

I leaned over to him and whispered, "Thanks again." He nodded. There was plenty of quiet mumbling going on around my ex, but his words weren't clear.

During chemistry class, I tried to focus on Ms. Ellis's lecture. We were having our first lab experiment later in the week. I wasn't looking forward to that.

Getting wrapped up in the preparations made blocking Kyle out easy.

The bell rang. Zach sat patiently in his chair, waiting for me to get my materials together. Kyle walked behind us. I suppose my face said it all, because Zach bolted upright and swung around to my ex.

"So, are you two shackin' up now or something?" Kyle spat at us.

Trying not to shake my head, I thought, *Man . . . this guy's gutsy*.

Zach responded, calm and strong: "I hear Tatum's business is no longer your concern."

Jeez, Zach, why couldn't you just say no? I hid behind my bodyguard, waiting for their chitchat to be over. I, the chicken that I was, slowly poked my head around Zach to try and get a peek at Kyle's face. His face was as red as a tomato—he was absolutely pissed.

"Oh, is that so?" Kyle snarled.

Zach didn't bother to look back at me when he spoke. "Tate, are you ready to go now?"

"Yeah, thanks." I turned for the door with my head dropped. I heard Zach move behind me. Good. But then I heard Kyle storming up beside me to pass.

He shoved his elbow into my side as he came up next to me, mumbling, "Whore."

Ouch . . . I doubled over, holding my side. The pain caught my breath. He had gotten his elbow perfectly tucked under the front part of my ribs.

Zach reached around me and shoved Kyle, hard. Losing his balance, Kyle went flying out of the classroom toward two teachers chatting in the hall.

"Kyle, what are you doing? Stop horsing around and move on to your next class. These football players never know when to stop," the teacher chuckled.

Kyle caught his balance and glared back at us. I quickly stared at the ground again, but with a slight grin this time. Hot damn . . . Zach got him!

When we stepped out into the hall, Kyle yelled back at Zach, "Good luck. She doesn't like putting out anyway."

Zach touched my shoulder. "Are you okay?"

"Yeah, I'll survive. Despite everything that went on today, I think it went quite well."

"What? Are you serious?" Zach gawked at me.

"Well, yeah, I am . . . all things considered." What was Zach's problem? I'd just escaped, that was all. Even if I only escaped because of him. I was happy.

"Considering what, Tate? Considering the underwear hanging from your locker door for all to see?—"

Gosh. He was mad.

"—Or maybe the sign he wrote? Or, wait, better yet—how about the jab . . ."

After he finished, he just looked away and shook his head. On our way back to my locker, I couldn't help but think. Zach was right. If Kyle didn't like me, then why couldn't he just leave me alone?

"Stop kidding yourself, Tate." He stepped off to the side of my locker.

I worked my combination, glancing up at his dark, angry eyes.

After school, heading for our buses, I said, "Will you call me sometime tonight? I need to talk to you, and not at school."

"Sure, I'll call in a little while."

I thanked him again for being my private bodyguard for the day.

He chuckled. "Anytime . . . but just for you. I'll talk to you soon."

I was just about to board my bus when I realized he was coming back over to me. Within seconds, he was holding my waist and pulling my body into his. I was shocked, but willing to let anything he did happen.

"Tate," he breathed.

I said nothing, trying to swallow the lump in my throat. He was reading my eyes. His hand felt great on my waist—so soft and gentle, a nice hold. I bit my lip, trying to figure out what to say. "Zach, I should get on the bus now."

His arm dropped to his side. "Of course, I'll call you soon."

I turned my body away while I kept my head looking back at him. Gosh . . . he was so intense. Scary that I liked that.

I knew damn well something just happened out there. Now what was I supposed to say to him when he called?

I ran inside the house and threw my stuff on the bed—I'd learned my lesson about leaving my things lying around the house. I let Gizmo outside and ran back to my room.

In a panic, waiting for Zach to call, I ran every possibility through my head.

This would be intense with him. Zach had proven he was passionate.

Okay, so at some point Zach might want to kiss me again. If he was more forceful about a kiss than he was today and I said no, would he back off and leave it at that? I was too scared to take the chance, but I did like him. He was so nice and considerate. His actions today said he liked me enough to sacrifice a fight with Asshole Football Player. I couldn't be stupid about what boys really wanted. I'd ignored the signs with Kyle. I couldn't allow myself another error with Zach. Or any guy for that matter. But not every guy was a rapist.

I walked over to my floor mirror and looked at the new Tatum. "Look in there and tell me you're not afraid of guys or of dating someone. That the next one won't be another Asshole Football Player."

Of course I was afraid, but I was pretty sure Zach was different. He was soft. Sincere. Caring. He didn't appear to be after just one thing. And the way he'd stuck up for me . . . you just don't do those things unless you care deeply for a person. Right? Of course, I'd thought Asshole Football Player cared too—

Kyle was in my face—*"Did you really think you could tease me this long and not give me something . . . I make you sick? You fucking bitch, you owe me . . . "* It all came rushing back . . .

The phone rang. I blinked and turned away from the mirror, darting for the nightstand.

"Hello," I said, slightly out of breath.

"Hi, it's Zach. Is this a good time?"

"Sure, now is good."

"Well, what did you want to talk to me about? Is everything okay?"

"Oh, everything is fine. I just wanted to talk to you about today. Us."

"Us? What do you mean, *us*?"

I was caught off guard, I hadn't expected him to say that. *Shoot, I'd just assumed he liked me. Dang it, maybe he doesn't. No, he wouldn't have done what he did at the buses if he didn't, right?* "Well, I don't really know how to say this, but let me start by saying I really like you as a friend, and I don't want to lose that. But I'm afraid that I may have given you the wrong impression today. You're a really nice guy, and words can't even express how much I appreciate everything you did for me, but I'm just not sure how—"

"Tate, I think you're getting upset over nothing. I understand."

"Oh."

"Yeah, I like you as a friend and want to keep it like that too . . . but I also can't lie about my feelings for you. And when I kissed your cheek . . . I know, I know, I said it was just for show and that it didn't mean anything—and I didn't mean for it to. We seemed right; it felt right. I know you felt it too."

"Zach . . . that's very nice of you, but I'm afraid of where this is going." Crap, of course I felt it. And that was one of the many things I feared. I didn't want to be known as the girl who dated one guy and the next day was with another.

There was a long, uncomfortable pause where neither of us said anything. I'd screwed up already.

"You're right. Just friends, I'll take it."

"So, then we're okay? Just good friends?" I asked.

"Yes, good friends."

Silence.

Why did I have him call me to just make it clear we were friends? That was obvious.

"Tatum Duncan, are you okay?"

"What . . . yeah, why? Of course I'm okay." *No, I don't think I am. Zach, you'd be smart to stop this and run in the other direction.*

"That is what you want, right, just friends?"

"I don't know, maybe, I just . . . well . . ." Well, crap, maybe I liked the idea of us. He made me feel good.

Zach was chuckling. "All right, let me tell you how I feel."

How he felt? Guys didn't tell anyone how they felt. Hmmm . . .

"I've liked you since the seventh grade. Being with you all day just confirmed to me that I have real feelings for you. Tatum, I want you to go out with me so we can spend our free time together. You have no idea how much willpower it takes for me to simply hold your waist and not kiss you. We would be great together—"

I cleared my throat without thinking. He was going right where I'd hoped he'd go, and now I didn't want to hear it. I was so fricking messed up. Why was it when he said what I wanted to hear, I wanted to run?

"Yes?" he said.

"Nothing, go ahead, I'm listening. There was just something in my throat—dry air." Like a frickin' dagger. I needed to receive the idiot-of-the-year award.

"Homecoming is coming up soon. Would you want to go with me?"

Well, why don't you just put my head in the door and slam it a few times; it may hurt less than this. Remember the last dance you went to? That turned out smashing.

After the last dance, I'd been scared shitless that Kyle would find out I'd kissed Zach and break up with me. Uhh, maybe that was what should have happened? That could have saved me. "Um. I'm not sure. Can I get back with you on that?"

"Of course. I'd never force you to do anything you didn't want to do. And just to make it clear, we would go just as friends. Unless you say otherwise. Tate, you call the shots."

I laughed out loud. Being the one to control

anything in my life was a joke. "Thanks, Zach. I appreciate it."

After we hung up, I grabbed a drink in the kitchen, then went back to my room to do chemistry homework. That class was going to be a hard one for me. Nonetheless, I had to get my grades back up. There was still time to correct the deterioration of my GPA caused by dating Kyle the previous semester. Dating a guy that only had to keep a 2.0 meant a lack of focus on studying. Lucky for me, though, there was still enough time before I began applying for scholarships.

I was getting comfy in bed to read about the first lab's safety precautions when I realized where my life stood at the moment. Although my emotions had been put through the ringer lately, I suddenly felt at ease. No boyfriend to worry about or hate. Exactly what I wanted—freedom and control.

I wanted guy friends I could feel comfortable with—talk to, go out with, and maybe even flirt with, like Zach. I liked Zach a lot, and the idea of us was exciting. All I wanted was to be a normal teenage girl again.

While I was reading step one, the phone rang again.

"Hello?"

"Hey, it's Val. What happened today?"

I took a deep breath; I was so tired. "Well, you're not going to believe how lucky I got."

"Really? I'm dying here, you have to tell me everything from the very beginning to the end. Go."

I chuckled at her. "Jeez, am I being timed or something?"

It took me a whole twenty-five minutes to update

her.

When I heard Gizmo barking, I knew my sister would be barging through the door any minute. Sure enough, I heard Toni and her girlfriend, Brittany, run inside.

Brittany yelled, "I'm a guest, I get the bathroom first."

The curse of one bathroom. I counted my blessings that I got home before anyone else.

"I'm smaller—I have a harder time holding it," Toni shouted back.

"Val, can you hold for a minute?" I opened my door and yelled, "Come on, girls, do what I did with my friends. Half and half. Your butts are small enough. Toni gets one side. Britt the other. Problem solved."

I looked down at Toni's surprised little face.

"What are you waiting for, Ton? Get in there. And keep it down outside my door. I'm on the phone. Go do your arguing somewhere else."

"Your hair, Tatey. Mommy is going to—"

"Yeah. Yeah. I know." I shut my door and picked up with Val where I had left off.

"So, this Zach guy . . . you swear you don't like him?" Valerie asked.

"What does that mean?"

"Well, I'm just saying, he sounds like a nice guy, and he clearly likes you—"

"That's just it. I do like him. And the friendship is already there. When he waited for me today, well, yeah. He totally looked sexy. I mean, he is sexy. God help me. So yeah, I guess you could say that I do like him. All that said, something's not right. I don't know what it is. It's just . . . I don't know." I took a deep breath. "I don't need to be with anyone right now. You know what I mean? I need more time than two days."

"I do, and I'm really glad to hear it, actually."

"Really, you're glad?"

"Yeah, what are you doing this weekend?" Valerie seemed to switch gears on me.

"I'm not thinking about the weekend yet. I still have to get through four more days of school with Asshole Football Player. And not to mention, my mom still hasn't seen my hair."

༄༄༄

Just as I hung up the phone, Gizmo started barking again.

Crap, Mom and Dad were home already.

"Toni, Mom and Dad are home. Get your homework out before they walk in the door."

It was time to own up to my haircut. I stood smack dab in the middle of the living room and waited for Mom to look at me. Dad came through the side door and walked down to the basement, but he wasn't the one I was worried about. As expected, Mom came in the front door.

I straightened my back and held my head high.

Mom closed the door behind her. She lifted her head . . . I met her stare . . . her face collapsed . . . she fell back into the closed door, flinging her hand over her heart.

That did it. I'd given my mother the heart attack she'd always said I would cause.

Hysterical was an understatement for my mom's reaction. "Why would you do this to your long, beautiful hair?"

"'Cause. I needed a change," I said. She did not

want to know the truth. Convenient, since I didn't want to tell anyone the truth anyway.

"You change your nail polish. You change your shoes. You don't chop your hair off like an idiot. Now look at you." She shook her head in disgust.

"What? I look like an idiot 'cause my hair is short?"

"I didn't say that. I just better not see you doing anything stupid again. Go to your room for the night. I can't stand to look at you like that."

That was me getting off easy. Because god knew I was bringing the world to an end! All because of a haircut. Wow. I knew not telling her the truth about what had happened was the right thing. She'd never understand. Nor did she ever know what to "do with" me. I guess to her, I was an idiot.

CHAPTER 14

The next morning, I scanned the bus unloading area for Zach. He wasn't here. The bus arrived much later than yesterday, but I'd hoped he would be around again. Then again, he owed me nothing.

When I got closer to my locker, I could see Zach waiting for me. He spotted me approaching and stood up, smiled, and quickly glanced away.

I stepped up to my locker and turned the combination dial.

"I wondered if you were coming at all today," Zach said.

"Unfortunately, I have no control over my bus driver." I swapped notebooks and books from my locker. "Whew, it looks like Asshole Football Player didn't put anything in my locker today." Changing the subject, I said, "I'm kinda surprised you're here. I wasn't sure if you'd . . . you know."

"I'll always stay by you. But do you want me to leave?"

My cheeks had instant rouge. "Of course not. I just wouldn't dream of asking you to do the same thing two days in a row. And, by the way . . . I still feel bad about dragging you into this." Zach backed up when I closed my locker. I gave it a quick tug to make sure it was locked. "Shall we?"

Zach stepped next to me. "We shall and don't apologize. I enjoy being with you, even if you're not interested in me like I am in you."

My head jerked toward him faster than a rubber band snapping. That wasn't true. "I didn't say that."

"Oh, calm down. I know. I know. I won't mention it again."

"You better not." I looked away. For once in my life, I wanted things to slow down.

Who knew how much control Zach had over his feelings? The last thing I wanted was to be around another guy who couldn't control his sexual cravings. Could Zach really want to be in a boyfriend-girlfriend commitment, though? I was damaged goods. Of course, he didn't know that, but he knew that I'd been dating Asshole Football Player. Sixteen years old and damaged goods . . . who wanted that? Hell, I didn't even want that.

"So, did you think about homecoming yet?" Zach asked.

"Ummm." I stalled, not knowing how to say I was afraid of going to another dance.

"That's okay, never mind."

I looked up at him as we stopped by the door of my first hour. He stood there facing me with his shoulder resting against the wall. He slouched down to be closer to my eye level.

"Of course I will. But only as a friend," I said.

"Sure, just as good friends, and nothing more," he confirmed.

Zach sighed loudly, whispering my name as he did so. "Tate-umm." He said it with such yearning.

Crap . . . was he wanting to kiss me?

I didn't move for Zach's lips, because the football jersey storming toward us caught my attention. And take two—Kyle elbowed me in the side again.

Kyle muttered something and kept walking. He ground his teeth together making it hard to understand, but I knew he had called me a bitch.

I slouched forward. "You idiot," I grunted. The pain was sharp, like he'd taken an ice pick and stabbed me in between my ribs.

Zach threw his books down and went after Kyle.

"Zach . . . no . . . let it go. Please." But he didn't. Zach caught up to Kyle and reached over the front of his shoulder, holding him back to slug one solid punch—"Hey, Kyle, how are ya?"

Kyle was flung forward.

With Zach's head turned to the side, I focused on his lips. "Touch her again, I dare ya," Zach whispered.

Kyle held his back where Zach hit.

Zach jogged back over to me. "Tate, are you okay?"

I couldn't help but cry. "No. That idiot. I'm so fed up with him." I rubbed my side, thinking it would work out the sting. But seeing Zach go after him, protecting me, had instantly made me feel better.

Zach softly wiped the tears from under my eyes, and said, "I know. Don't cry, hon, you're smearing your artwork."

"My artwork? Whatchya talking about?" Tears ran down my face.

"Your mascara's running." He seemed unsure of whether or not to wipe my cheek.

The warmth of his support spun around me faster

than a sewing machine's spool. "Of course . . . my art." I chuckled. He was so darn cute. So why wasn't I giving us a chance? I'd given Kyle a chance, even though he couldn't have cared less about me. And here Zach was, a normal, sexy guy. What was my problem?

Just then, the two-minute warning bell rang.

I was a hot mess, swiping tears and sniffling. "I need Tylenol. I feel like I've been living off of these recently."

I shuffled things around inside my purse to find the Tylenol and quickly popped two in my mouth. "Zach, I'm so sorry. I don't understand why he won't just leave me alone—"

Before I could finish, Zach pulled me into his arms. He put one hand on the back of my head and gently held me there up against his chest. Ahhh . . . it was so nice. I could stay against his chest forever. He accepted me for who I was. A half-shaved head. My vintage sweaters—or, as the "it" girls called them, *old sweaters*. The black combat boots that hated leaving my feet. He didn't mind any of my quirks. And the best thing, in my opinion, were his kisses. He made my insides squirm. I couldn't deny the affection between us.

He pulled back and dropped one hand from around me and placed it on the side of my head, cradling. *Ohhh crap, here we go.*

He pulled my face toward his. I watched his eyes softly close. I swiftly but discreetly pulled back. "Zach, don't. Not here."

He dropped his hands from my face and whispered ashamedly, "I'm sorry, I . . . I—"

"I know, but the bell is about to ring." I rolled my

eyes. "Everyone is staring at us."

"Yeah, I suppose you're right."

Zach put his hands on my shoulders. "Sorry, just friends. I'll tattoo that into my head."

"Oh, don't go and get a tattoo on my account."

"So, you don't like tattoos?"

Weird thing to ask. "Not particularly, but I guess it's fine." He dropped it, and so did I. Put that on the *weird-things-to-ask* list.

Just like clockwork, after I got home, Val called, requesting a full update. She wasn't as excited to hear about the Zach thing.

"What do you mean by *he gently grabbed your face and tried to kiss you*? Did you want him to kiss you? It sounds like you did."

I sat on the bar stool in the kitchen with the memory fresh in my head. "I guess I did, but it doesn't matter. Is there a problem? Why do you sound so hostile?"

"I'm not. I just thought you didn't have real feelings for him."

"I never said I don't have feelings for him. Never. What's the problem? He's sweet . . . *and* he's been really protective lately. Remember, I have no one else there to help me out with Asshole Football Player. And not to mention if it wasn't for Zach right now, there's no telling how much Asshole Football Player would have hurt me."

It was time to examine how much input my friends had in my social life.

The rest of the week went off without a snag.

Well, almost.

Wednesday: No advances from Zach, and nothing from Kyle.

Thursday: No advances from Zach, and nothing from Kyle.

Friday: Not so lucky with Zach.

During lunch on Friday, Andi asked, "Do you want to spend the night tonight? My mom will be at work all night. My stepdad will be home, but he stays in his room anyway."

"I'll ask my parents when they get home after work and call ya," I said.

As Zach and I walked to forth hour, he was unusually quiet.

"Are you okay? Is something wrong?"

Zach avoided meeting my eyes. "I'm fine. I'm just pouting a bit."

"Pouting? Why on earth are you pouting?" Too funny, because if there was one thing Zach Bertano did not do, it was pout.

He looked at me with sad eyes. "Andi beat me to it."

I refrained from bursting into laughter. "Oh, did you want me to spend the night too?"

Rolling his eyes. "Ha. Ha. Ha."

I couldn't stop laughing at him. "I'm sorry, I don't know why I find this so funny."

"It's okay. I was just hoping to do something with you tonight because I have to work Saturday." He looked over at me.

His eyes said he wanted more than a movie or dinner . . .

We went to class without another word. What was I supposed to say?

After school, we said our goodbyes: *See ya Monday—Have a good weekend.*

Right as I turned for my bus, Zach stopped me.

"Tate, wait a minute."

He grabbed my arm and spun me around—reminiscent of ballroom dancing.

"That's it . . . I'm sorry, I can't help myself."

"What—"

But it was too late. He grabbed me around my waist and pulled me to him with such force a puff of air escaped my mouth with an *oomph*.

My body stiffened, and I found myself straining my head away from him.

Zach stopped and stared at me. He gave me the lost-puppy look. "Tatum? What's wrong? Why do you look like I'm about to hit you?"

"Huh?" I relaxed, seeing he was right. My body stood more rigid than an iceberg. Letting myself relax more, I rested my head on his chest. "Sorry. Reflex. I overreacted."

Zach pulled me into a soft embrace. "What happened to you?" He moved close to the side of my head. "I swear on my mother's life, I'd never hurt you. I'd rather die than let anything happen to you."

All I heard was—love, forever, safety. And he meant it.

I looked up at him, meeting his eyes. "Thank you."

His lips parted, then closed. He didn't let me out of his hold, but he lowered his hands and looked in my eyes. His eyes sang, "Trust in me." And I did.

I trusted him more than anybody.

Around Kyle, I'd never felt at ease. With Zach, I'd trust him if he told me to get in a room filled with snakes, saying they wouldn't bite. I'd do it.

And I could do this. Not every guy was going to be like my first boyfriend.

Going with what felt natural to me, I angled my head and moved toward his mouth. Zach exhaled. His lips met mine.

The moment I felt the warmth and love, he wasn't the only participant.

This was similar to the first kiss he'd given me. First kiss anyone had given me. This was different, though. I wasn't dating anyone. I could kiss whoever I wanted.

And Zach was the guy.

Letting my stuff drop to the ground, I reached up and locked my arms behind his neck.

He bear-hugged me, squeezing me into him. Tighter. Tighter.

In that moment I wanted nothing but for him to keep making me feel the way he was. I could feel every tingling volt traveling from my toes—up my legs—between my legs—up my torso and up the back of my head, causing my scalp to tickle. It was slightly embarrassing feeling my breasts react next.

In Zach's effort to mold our bodies into one, he slowly raised me off the ground. My chest rose and fell—I was breathing heavily.

I didn't want him to put me down. That's when I noticed his scent—light and expensive.

That alone drove me straight to the asylum.

Then out of the blue, I felt someone watching us. Why would I feel guilty? But I opened my eyes and saw Christy standing right behind Zach, which was why I began to slide back down to the ground. This was not a kiss to share with an audience.

My hands released the back of his head; I hadn't noticed my fingers were playing with his hair. Christy was so shocked that her eyes looked as if they would pop out of her head.

"Um . . . sorry to interrupt, Tatum. But our bus is going to leave any second now."

Zach and I slowly parted. "I gotta go," I breathed next to his mouth. Our foreheads were touching. Zach opened his eyes. We stared at each other.

He put me down and took a half a step back. His chest was pumping the same way mine was.

Christy grabbed my stuff from the ground and shoved it into my stomach. I couldn't care less. I was happy at the moment. Was that what it was supposed to be like between boyfriend and girlfriend? Because Kyle and I never came close to what Zach and I felt just then. Never.

"I'll see you Monday, Zach," I said in a flirtatious manner. Christy was pulling me away from him. If I wanted to go home, it was best she took control.

For his kiss made me lose my modesty. My common sense. My fricking *mind*.

Zach was displaying a sultry grin himself. "Have fun this weekend, Tate." Then he ran his tongue along his lips. Those perfect. Kissable. Lips.

My heart was beating faster than a racehorse's, giving me the adrenaline to throw myself out of the gate. I hadn't thought twice before kissing Zach back. I'd thought once and dived in. How far would I have gone? Secretly, I was glad she was pulling me away from him. Otherwise, I didn't know what would have happened next.

CHAPTER 15

Christy and I took our usual seats on our bus. Before my butt got situated, she reminded me of my mother. And not in a good way.

"What in the world . . . are you and Zach Bertano getting together now?"

"Shhh. You weren't supposed to see that." I stared out the window. Feeling the glow I was wearing proudly on my cheeks. For once in my life, a guy was genuinely interested in me.

I could feel my heart beat faster as his kiss ran through my head.

"Well, let me tell ya something . . . maybe I wasn't . . . but what about the couple of hundred or so kids that just did? You guys locked together in clear view of at least five buses. How come you haven't told me about you two?" she chastised.

"Maybe because there's really not an 'us two.'" I couldn't look at her and lie to her face.

The truth was that after I'd kissed him, I wanted to kiss him again, and soon. The experience had left me wondering how things could develop between the two of us. Jesus. That felt good. So passionate. He made me feel beautiful. Yes ma'am, I needed to see him again.

"How could there not be, if you're locking lips in the back of school? And you guys didn't just lock lips, Tate. It was like you were molding your bodies as one from head to toe."

"Shh. I don't want the whole bus to hear." She needed to lower her voice that second.

"Oh, that's original. You don't want the whole bus to hear us, but it's okay for half the school to see you?"

She was right. We'd done that in front of how many people? Damn it. "What does it matter to you? And it wasn't half the school, so stop exaggerating. Besides, I'm sure you've done worse with Eric, and who knows what you'll do with this Ben."

"Uhhh . . . that was unnecessary."

"Oh, really? What's unnecessary is how I've been through hell recently, and here you are yelling at me for kissing the guy who has kept me not only sane, but safe. You know most of what Asshole Football Player's done to me. But you have no clue what it's like for me being in that hell box all day with him. And you're going to get all pissy because I gave my guy friend a goodbye kiss? I liked the way Zach made me feel out there. So what? Get over it."

For once Christy didn't have anything to say to me. We'd both said what we'd wanted, or at least I had.

As we got off the bus, Christy quietly said, "Well, maybe a goodbye kiss isn't such a big deal . . . but don't you realize how many people saw the two of you?"

"I know, I know. But it was just a kiss. Can we not make a big deal out of it? Please?"

She looked at me, then away. I couldn't decide if

she was afraid to make eye contact or if she was thinking before she spoke. Which would be a first.

"I suppose, but you're giving him a different impression than what you've said this whole week, right?"

If I admitted my intentions had changed, then she'd shut up about it. Yes, she was right. "I know, and I think it's too late. If I wanted to keep things between us just friends, I know kissing him screwed everything up. But I'm confused." That was my story and I was sticking to it. I looked at Christy, begging her, "Please, tell me it's okay to be curious with him. I've never felt anything like this. I'm just . . . I'm just trying to figure it all out. Why am I not allowed that?"

Later that evening, over at Andi's house, we were in her bedroom.

She kept busy trying on a bunch of new tops her mother had bought. I kept DJing their Barry Manilow record collection.

Andi was looking in the mirror at how her new shirt made her boobs look. I always joked that, compared to hers, mine were as big as M&M's—and the peanut ones were pushing it. Andi's were the size of watermelons. I didn't want boobs that big; I wouldn't be able to walk. Now the image of me with monstrous boobs, hunched over and walking with a cane, flashed in my mind. No, not that big. But just a little bigger than plain M&M's would have been nice.

"So, I got a call from Tommy. Can you turn the Copa down, please? Why must you turn him up so loud?" Andi yelled.

I turned it down. I guess we didn't share the same amount of love for Barry Manilow.

"Man . . . I haven't talked to him in ages. How is he?"

Tommy was one of Andi's friends from in grade school. He was half Mexican, with beautiful clear skin and jet-black hair. He was taller than she, which was good. A cute guy, but not my type.

Andi was taking her shirt off and putting another one on.

She looked back at me. "He said he saw you and Zach Bertano locking bodies out at the buses after school." She tossed me that shirt. "Here, you wanna try it on? It'll fit you better." It landed on my lap.

"What in the world . . . what's the big deal? Yeah, so what? I kissed Zach. Well, actually, he kinda kissed me first. That doesn't mean it should be spread around like wildfire, my lord. And your tops will not fit me." I tossed it on her bed.

Andi sat next to me. "Tatum, I do not know why you think you're so small. I wish I had your size. Trust me, these things are a monstrosity—they should have their own zip code. And for Mr. Bertano and you . . . don't ya think you should have kissed Zach in a more private place, then?"

I jumped off the bed and started pacing with my arms flying everywhere. "What is the big deal? Why am I getting so much crap for this?" I stopped and looked at her. "Okay, you know what, I was curious. He kissed me and I got into it. I mean . . . am I to be crucified because I let a guy kiss me?" Damn, if I'd known this was going to happen, I would have thought twice. I flung the shirt on, and we both stared at the fit.

She shook her head. "Sorry. These damn things already stretched it out. It'll shrink. Put it in the dryer—it's cotton. And calm down." She came up behind me and started to rub my shoulders. "I think it's kinda romantic. You and Zach."

"What? Really? You do? Romantic?" I turned around.

She sat back down on her bed. "I do. Of course, I wish I'd seen you guys. With how he's been with you all week, especially at lunchtime? He really likes you."

As she was talking, I started to get excited, recalling how he'd defended me when Kyle hit me. How he'd reassured me that there was no excuse for my first boyfriend to treat me that way, that I'd never deserved it. Not once did he ditch me or complain about anything I'd done. And then when he'd kissed me earlier, I'd felt that spark. I mean, Zach was the sexiest guy in school, hands down. Tall, dark and . . . different. Wait. Different?

"Uh, hello, Tate, are you okay?"

I snapped back to reality. "Oh yeah, so you think he really cares about me?"

"Are ya blind? Everyone can see that." She twisted her mouth. "So, whatcha gonna do?"

"Oh, I don't know. Did Tom say anything else?"

"He said how it looked like Zach was really hot for you."

Crap. Why didn't I think about where we were? 'Cause I was in the moment? I need to stop beating myself up over this. That's why it's called 'in the moment.'

"He also said that when Zach grabbed you, all the girls on his bus sat up to look out. Jealous. He said they watched you two from the moment you got out there. Sounds as if you've been a good soap opera since Monday after school." Andi laughed.

"Okay, I think I got the point. Thank you very much." I mumbled, "This is so embarrassing. I didn't even stop to think about people watching us."

"Clearly. I wish someone would say how good me and Tommy looked together, but you know that will never happen. Don't worry about it. You know, there are worse things in life than people going on about you and Zach."

"Yeah, I suppose you're right."

Tommy was Andi's secret love. She had loved him without his knowledge for years. Andi crawled up in her bed and rested her back against her headboard.

"I just know Asshole Football Player will hear about this, and when he does, it won't do me any good. It'll give him another excuse to attack me."

"Oh, yeah, I didn't think of that. But he shouldn't be attacking anyone."

"This sucks." I plopped myself onto her bed again. "What do I do?"

"Aww. Poor Tatum Duncan. What is she to do with her boy issues? She has Zach Bertano kissing her. Oh, poor baby."

"Oh, shut up. And what's that supposed to mean?"

"It means that you have a nice guy who adores you and a guy who's jealous because this guy likes you. I wish I had a couple of guys fighting over me."

If she only knew what Kyle had done to me, she wouldn't have said that. "Well, if I could change places with you, I'd do it in a heartbeat. Not that I don't like Zach. I do. It's just . . . well, I could use a break. What I'd like is to have fun for a while without any stupid commitments or fighting with Asshole Football Player. All I did for months was fight with him, make up, fight again. I'm tired."

"I suppose, but I don't feel sorry for you."

I didn't ask for anyone to feel sorry for me. But maybe if she knew how much I'd valued my virginity and that Kyle had taken it from me after beating the crap out of me, she wouldn't want to be me.

Andi jumped out of bed. "Let's go upstairs and get some food."

I followed her up to the kitchen.

"Don't you want anything else besides tea, Tate?"

"No thanks, I'm fine. I had dinner before I left."

Just then the phone rang.

"It's probably my mom checking in—hold on." Andi answered, "Hello?"

There was a pause. When she turned to me, her eyes went wild.

"What's wrong?" I mouthed.

"Yeah, no problem, Zach. She's right here."

Oh, crap.

Andi covered the phone. "It's Zach. He wants to talk to you."

I covered the phone and whispered, "What does he want?"

"I don't know. He just apologized for interrupting."

Uncovering the phone, I took a deep breath and said a Hail Mary, then answered "Hello?"

"Tatum? It's Zach."

"I know, is everything okay?"

"I hope so. I'm calling to see if you're getting any of the same reactions I'm getting from our goodbye at school today. It sounds like we caused quite a stir."

I tilted the phone out so Andi could listen in. She put her head to mine.

"Well, I'm not sure what you're getting, but I've gotten a *little* feedback."

Andi smacked my shoulder.

"Ow, what was that for?" I whispered.

"Tate, I just wanted to apologize. I didn't even think about all the people that would be watching. I hope you're not getting too much crap for it."

"Oh, no. Not too bad. Andi reminded me that it could be worse."

"Uh, okay . . . I suppose it could be worse."

"Oh, no, I didn't mean it like that. I'm sorry, that's not what I meant."

"No need to apologize. You've told me how you feel and I've told you how I feel, and that's it. We kissed, so what? I think everybody needs to mind their own business."

"Exactly. How bad are their lives when all they talk about is ours? Sad."

Zach started chuckling. "Thanks. I was a little concerned that you were grossed out by me. Especially if you were getting crap from people."

"Who's given you a hard time or mentioned it to you?"

Andi was still listening attentively.

"Really? You want to know?"

"Yeah, if people are talking about me, I'd like to know what they're saying. Don't I have that right?"

"Sure, Tate. For starters, everyone on the bus was high-fiving me when I got on. Then Tyler called me about it when I got home. Then after that—"

"Got it, thanks."

"Are you mad? I mean, you asked."

I couldn't respond. Because my mother taught me if you didn't have anything nice to say, then don't say anything at all. There, she couldn't claim I never listened to her.

"Say something, Tate."

Andi started giggling and covered her mouth. I tried to elbow her. "I'm not mad at you. I'm mad at myself. Do you know what this is going to mean for me and Asshole?"

"Oh. I see your point. That wasn't my intention at all. Easy fix—I'll stay with you all next week, too."

"How convenient." Why would he mock the situation?

"Well, I'll let you go. Tyler's coming over soon."

When Tyler and Zach went out, the rumors going around school the following Monday always involved the police.

"Are you two staying there? You're not going to be driving around, are you?"

"Tatum Duncan, are you worried about me?"

"Yes, I am. I don't want you hurt or in trouble. You and Tyler don't make the best decisions when you're together. I need my bodyguard in one piece on Monday."

"I'm really looking forward to guarding your body."

I cleared my throat, wanting to kick someone . . . Andi, she was laughing. "Zach, stop it. Be careful tonight and I'll see ya Monday."

"All right, see ya. Oh, before I forget, tell Andi I said thanks for letting me interrupt."

"I'll tell her. Bye now." When I put the phone back on the receiver, Andi burst into laughter. I could have kicked her. "Oh, you think this is just peachy keen, don't you?"

"Yes, actually, I do. How do you do it? You

always seem to get yourself into these situations."

We went back to her bedroom downstairs. Andi sat at her vanity and ate her food. I went back to the bed and sat down after I'd put my drink on her dresser.

Andi finally broke the silence between us. "Tatum, he's so cute—if you get tired of him, pass him on to me. Before I thought he was quiet, but now that I've talked to him, I like him. He's so sweet." Andi took another bite of her corn dog.

"Like I said, you can have them all."

CHAPTER 16

The next morning I went home to work on my laundry.

About one o'clock, Val called like she'd said she would and invited me over. My weekend had quickly turned into a sleepover marathon.

Once at Valerie's house, I followed her up the steps to her bedroom.

"So, I see you're still wearing the wristbands."

I glanced down at them. "For a while longer. I didn't even tell you what the asshole did this week to my side. I'll never get rid of him at this point. Or at least, that's how it feels." I threw my stuff down on her bed.

"What? You mean Kyle hurt you again?"

"For Christ's sake, will everyone stop saying his name?"

"Oh, sorry, forgot." Val dropped her head.

She was next to get the updated story. Somehow I always forgot she didn't go to our school. "That's why I felt if Zach wanted a kiss, by god I'd give him a kiss."

Val almost fell off her bed. "You kissed him? Please don't tell me you kissed him on the lips? Oh god. You know that's complicating things, don't ya?"

"Well, thanks for understanding." Not again . . . my patience was wearing thin on that subject. After another long explanation, she seemed to calm down quite a bit.

Val's family had been out to dinner for about a half an hour when the phone rang.

"Hello? Oh, hi, Scott. Yeah, Tate's here. We're just watching a movie."

There was a pause, and Val was giving me a crooked look. I looked back at her with a smirk. She was cracking me up.

Val rolled her eyes. "No, I don't think that's a good idea right now. It appears as if our little Tate has found a private bodyguard at school." Pause. "No, I know, that's good. But you don't understand. This bodyguard and her have kissed *and* . . . they're going to homecoming together." Val kept rolling her eyes.

I couldn't let them talk about me like I wasn't even there, so I grabbed the phone out of her hands. "Scott, it's Tatum. Is there a problem?"

Val was doing a jumping chicken dance, trying to get the phone back.

"Oh, hey, Tate, how are you?"

"Oh, don't even. I want to know why you and Val are going on about my business."

"Now calm down, we were just talking. Nothing important, I asked how your week went with Kyle. That's all."

I grinded my teeth. "Really? Well, you can ask me. And it went fine . . . thanks to Zach. If it weren't for him, I would have more than just some bruises on my side—"

"I swear, if I run into that guy . . . ever, he may

have a few fucking bruises of his own—"

"Great, so Val told you."

Val stopped jumping and turned away from me. "I didn't tell him, just that Kyle attacked you."

I gave Val's backside venomous looks. "I should have known. That's okay. But that's what I'm saying, if it wasn't for Zach, I'd be in really bad shape."

"But you're going to homecoming with this guy?"

"You know what, how about this . . . I'll pay to put an article about my private life in the *Suburban Journal*, then you and everyone else in North County will have what you need to know in writing. Bye, Scott."

I turned to Val and tossed the phone in the air. Val stumbled to catch it.

In her doorway, I turned back to her. "I'll be downstairs grabbing a drink, and when I come back up I will not say or hear another word about Zach and me."

As I walked down the steps, I could hear Val saying, "Yeah, I think she's getting upset. Maybe we should forget about it for now. Tate needs to figure things out with this Zach guy first. And I told you to play dumb about the Asshole Football Player thing—"

The farther I walked down the steps, the less I heard. I'd heard all I needed to. It sounded as if they would probably stop whatever they'd been scheming. I wished people would let me figure out my own damn life. Nosy-ass friends.

I poured myself a glass of iced tea, wondering what Zach was up to. He'd wanted to do something the night before, since he had to work tonight. I hadn't known he worked. What kind of friend was I?

I hadn't even thought of asking where.

"Why do I get this feeling you're out with Tyler? Why couldn't you ask me on a date tonight?"

"TATUM."

I didn't actually pee my pants, but it sure looked like it and felt like it with spilled tea down the front of me. "What in the world, Val?"

"What were you saying, Tatum? I thought not one more word about this Zach. Huh?"

I slammed the refrigerator door and glared at Val, who had her arms crossed and was tapping her foot on the floor as if I were the rude one.

"Okay, first of all, I'm soaking wet thanks to you. Two, you weren't supposed to be walking up on me without letting me know."

"So, the rule you put into place when you threw the phone at me applies to everyone but you?"

I slammed my empty cup on the counter, then wiped myself with paper towels. "I didn't throw the phone at you. I tossed it. You caught it, no harm done."

Val huffed, then grabbed towels to help wipe the floor up.

I'm not sure what set me off. Maybe it was the huff. "Fine. I was thinking about him. Let me get the cross and nails."

Valerie stood there unfazed, holding a dripping wet towel. "Oh no, you don't. You can pitch a fit, but it won't work with me, sweetie. We've been friends too long. Now, you said 'not another word,' then I come down here and you're babbling on about him. So, what is it between you two? Do you like him or not?"

I exhaled and dropped my head. This was

exhausting. "Like I've said. I'm curious right now. One part of me wants to see what could happen between us. But there's this huge complicating factor that tells me to stay away from him. Like there's something bad about him, real bad. And the frustrating thing is that I know this, I feel it, but when I'm with him and he touches me, something happens inside. This reservation doesn't exist. I can't explain it. It's . . . it's weird. It's like he makes me feel strong. Like I can do anything with him at my side. I know . . . hokey."

Not meeting my eyes, she exhaled and took a deep breath. "To be honest . . ." She then looked at me. "It's not hokey. Around you, I feel lighter. Like if Scott and I are fighting, I want to be around you. Maybe there's something about you that brings out a better me."

"Nope. No hokey going on here tonight," I said. We both laughed.

She walked around the island to me, putting her hand on my shoulder. "Look, maybe it's because there's just great energy between you two? Like we're on the same plane. Maybe you and this Zach have it. So if he makes you feel good, then who am I or anyone else to tell you to walk away from him? God knows you've been through enough shit with—"

"Don't say his name."

"Sorry. You know . . . it's time someone made you feel good about yourself."

"Jeez, isn't that the truth? Thanks." I felt the shakes starting again. Just the thought of Asshole Football Player sent my nerves into panic. My body ached from head to toe. The rug burns on my back felt as if they'd caught on fire. I tucked my hands behind me so Val wouldn't notice the shaking.

"So that's why you zoned out. Your grandma always encouraged you to meditate, looking as if you're just sitting there. But you were mumbling."

I looked at her and grinned. "Yeah, didn't realize it. I haven't done that in a while. Haven't done a lot of the self-awareness exercises Grandma taught me since she—" I couldn't say the D word.

"Anyway, back to Zach . . . I catch myself telling him things and then asking myself, why did I just tell him that? And the scary thing is, it feels completely natural with him. To be so open and honest with anyone, especially a boy . . . I can't explain it." I took a breath.

"I understand. And I say, to hell with everybody. You follow your heart this once."

Talking to Val was exactly what I needed to get refocused on myself. Healing and moving on. Didn't stop her, though, from asking me to please call the police to file a report. Definitely a friend of mine—she was so damn determined.

An hour later, we were lying in her bed, watching a movie. "I have to take these bands off. I'm so done with all of this."

I took them off. The bruising looked better. Val played with my new hair while we lay there relaxing the rest of the night, talking about my grandmother.

Val had met her a couple of times before she passed, so she loved hearing more stories about her. She especially liked reliving the story about the last time we left Grandma and Grandpa's house. Val had come along to keep me company while my family took care of a few last things before putting the house on the market. The atmosphere had been somber—

slumped shoulders and wet eyes. We were all about to pile in the van. My dad slammed the front door shut, double-checking the lock, then gently shut the storm door. Then he made sure that was shut snug. He walked off the front porch and toward the van. Before I got in, I glanced back at her door one last time. Suddenly, my grandparents' storm door flew wide open. My dad froze. My mom gasped. Dad slowly turned his head back to the door. He was clearly afraid of looking back.

I swallowed and said, "Dad, I think Grandma's coming with us."

The corners of his mouth spread upward. Then, just as suddenly, the door violently slammed shut. Val cursed under her breath in disbelief. My mom looked around to make sure we weren't too freaked out.

Dad turned back to the van. "Come on, Mom, and climb in next to Tate. Girls . . . Grandma's coming home with us."

Dad may have been joking, but I'd known she really was coming with us.

CHAPTER 17

Sunday afternoon, my laundry was piling up after I'd been gone all weekend. Trying to get homework and chores done seemed like the perfect time for the phone to ring.

"Hi, I saw your bedroom light on and assumed you were home. Can you talk?" Christy asked.

"Sure, how was last night? Did you go out with Ben?" I propped the phone between my head and shoulder so I could dust my room while we talked.

"I did, and you're not going to believe what I did. I asked him to go to homecoming with me. You don't think that's too forward, do ya?"

"Nah, girls ask guys all the time—you're fine. I wouldn't worry about that. So, what did he say?"

"Can you believe it, he said yes? Something crossed my mind, though."

"What's that?"

"I don't want to leave you out—"

I couldn't move.

"I mean, I know you and K—"

"Don't say his name," I shouted. Oh, god. That fucking name would not leave me alone.

"Sorry. You and Football Player definitely aren't going, and not sure if you want to go, but I'd hate to leave you by yourself."

I took a deep breath and then exhaled as I closed my eyes, forcing the shakes to stay away. "Chris, I'm going to tell you something, but I don't want you to say anything about it."

"Okay."

I opened my eyes. "Because Christy, I'd hate to have to pull your tongue out through the phone line—"

"Jesus Christ, Tate. I got it, I got it. Now are you going to tell me or what?"

"Plain and simple, I'm going to homecoming with Zach. So there's no need to worry about me, although that was mighty kind of you."

There was a long pause.

Christy mustered an, "Um, ah . . ."

"Thanks, so tell me more about Ben."

I worked on my laundry while Christy went on for half an hour, not taking a breath, telling me Ben's life story.

The TV news was on in the living room, and the moment the broadcast ended, my parents would go to bed. This would be a dreadful task for me, for the simple reason that I hated asking my parents for money—especially my dad—but I had to get another dress.

One foot in front of the other, straight into the lion's den.

Dad was in his recliner swivel chair, and Mom was on the couch.

"Mom, Dad . . . I wanted to talk to you about a dance that's coming up."

Mom's face narrowed. "Another dance? Well,

which one is this now?"

"Homecoming. It's next weekend. And unfortunately I need to get a dress." *Hold your breath. Hold it.*

"Huh, didn't you and Kyle know about this earlier?" my mom said, suddenly looking a bit more interested.

Please lord, give me the strength. "It's not him. I'm going with this guy, Zach."

"What do you mean, some guy Zach? Why aren't you going with Kyle?"

I never understood my mother. Since spring, she hadn't cared for Kyle, and now she was getting upset because he wasn't taking me. "We broke up. Last weekend. I've known Zach since seventh grade, and he asked me to go as friends. So, why not? I wasn't planning on going, but I thought it would be fun with a friend."

My dad took his eyes off the TV for a moment. "Cynthia, if she wants to go with some other guy, who cares? It's not as if you liked Kyle anyway."

My teeth ground together. I couldn't possibly tell my dad to call him Asshole Football Player.

I looked over at my mom and she had one eyebrow raised, looking suspicious. Her behavior made me wonder what she'd done as a teenager.

Take a breath and then just spit it out. "That leads me to my next question, do you think we could go get a new dress?"

On cue, Dad adjusted himself against the floral polyester seat. "Money, how much?"

"Oh, I don't know, maybe forty bucks could work."

My dad didn't care who I went with as long as he

didn't have to pay for it. My mom, on the other hand, cared who I went with, but always loved any excuse to get me dolled up.

"Well, Kenny, forty dollars isn't going to kill us. Sure, we can give you the money. We just can't do the car again. We don't have the money to do this every six months, Tatum. And that gives me an idea. It's about time you got a part-time job after this dance. I can get you hired on for the weekends at my place. The job won't interfere with your studies, and I think it's about time you start earning your own play money."

I would deal with the job thing later. "Fine. So, could someone take me to the mall this week? I'm sure there won't be much of a selection anymore, but I don't want to wear the same dress that I wore to the Sweetheart Dance."

Mom looked excited. I knew it was because she was delighted to go dress shopping again; she was such a dress junkie.

At my locker the next morning, not only was Zach waiting for me, but Andi was standing there talking to him. He wasn't facing Andi, though. He made eye contact with me through the crowd. When anyone stepped in our line of sight, Zach adjusted his stare around the moving students.

I had no clue what to do about him. Dismissing "our kiss" and not getting involved was probably the smart thing to do. But he really felt good, and not just because he was a good kisser. He felt natural to me. Damn it. I'd even told Val how comfortable I felt with him.

I stepped up to my locker. "Hey guys, how are

ya?" I asked them both.

Andi looked at me with a twinkle in her eye and a big grin on her face. "Fine. Just waiting for you."

Zach looked away from her and sighed, looking a bit put out.

"So, you guys are going to homecoming. Are ya gettin' a new dress, Tate?" Andi bounced.

"I am, actually. My parents are taking me out Friday. Zach, what are you wearing?"

Zach bent down to me, his eyes soft and gentle. "I'll wear something that'll go with anything you pick out. Don't worry."

Given how he typically dressed, I wasn't worried. I knew Zach would look handsome and perfect. I closed my locker and turned to Andi. "So, are you going to the dance?"

"I don't know yet. I asked Tommy this morning. He's thinking about it."

Wow. That would totally freak me out if I were her. He had to think about it? Yikes. "Well, I hope you go either way. It'll be fun."

Andi walked off with a spring in her step.

Zach gently rubbed the middle of my back. I flinched, ducking away from his touch. Not because I didn't want him to touch me, but because the rug burn was still there, although it was faint. All the visible marks on my body were diminishing. He dropped his hand.

"Oh, sorry. I didn't mean to—"

"Zach, you're fine. It's just a little sore. I slept wrong last night."

He let it go, but the look on his face said, *I know you're keeping something from me.*

At lunch, Andi was unbearable. Tommy had told

her yes. Maybe Tommy did think of her as more than just a friend. After all the years she'd spent pining for him, I hoped her waiting had paid off.

CHAPTER 18

October 1989

Saturday afternoon, it was time to get ready for the dance. Adrenaline was pushing me. It'd have to, since I hadn't slept well. In the shower was when it hit me: nervousness. My anxiety was a puzzle. If we were all friends, then why be so nervous? Then it happened: I imagined his lips coming for me.

Under the streaming water, I leaned on the wall in front of me. Zach's lips. *Breathe, Tatum, breathe.* Whew, just thinking about him made me hot. I reached down and made the water colder. Nothing helped.

What was wrong with me? *Damn it, Zach, why? Why am I still hesitant about you?* What could I be missing? Sometimes I felt like I couldn't read him. And when I recalled Grandma's words, I knew he was keeping something important from me. It was all there in his eyes, but what? He was mysterious, quiet, and even distant to everyone but me. Why me? And why the hell was I so fricking comfortable with him—like, imagining-him-in-the-shower-with-me comfortable? Oh, boy, this could be disastrous.

I was afraid that my hormones would take over if Zach tried to make a move. I didn't trust myself not to get caught up in the moment. Knowing Zach, there would be "a moment." I just told myself to stand strong and plant my feet and not budge.

In my bedroom, the radio was on. I made all the proper girly preparations for a date. My hair looked good—my bangs were calm, and the rest was shiny.

Six thirty-five and voila, I was ready. I was never early; tonight was starting off quite nicely. Standing in front of my floor-length mirror gave me the perfect view of my dress. The off-white strapless princess gown had a chiffon overlay, and toward the hem there were sequins with silver and cream beads arranged in a flower print. It was beautiful.

I got a drink of water and waited in the kitchen, alone.

"Are you ready? The dress really fits ya, Tate. I'm so glad you're not wearing those wristbands." Mom walked in.

That was the best I would get from her. She never hugged me or told me how pretty I looked. "Yeah, it's great."

"We got really lucky with this one. And who knew you would like a big puffy white dress? See, you can change your style without chopping your hair off."

"Well, I do like it. And we did get lucky. At least Dad liked the price too." Of course she had to sneak in a guilt trip.

The doorbell startled me, almost causing me to drop my cup. I tossed it into the sink. "I guess that's Zach." I headed toward the front door.

Toni hurried in to see who the new guy was. Fortunately for me, Dad was at the store. I just wished my mother could have been gone, too.

Just as we got to the hall, my mom stopped me. "If he starts drinking and smoking or driving crazy, you ask him to pull over to a 7-11 and call us. We'll come and get you. No funny stuff, do you hear me?"

"Yes, of course. I wasn't really thinking about anything funny, but okay—"

"*Tate.*"

"Mom, please. I get it."

We turned the corner. Toni was giggling and talking to Zach. The sight of him standing there took my breath away. Holy Mother Mary and Jesus, he looked like a sexy Italian male model, ready to strut the catwalk.

Zach looked up and instantly smiled. "Tate! Wow. You look great."

"Oh my lord, he's tall," my mom said, peering around me.

"Mom, please," I said through gritted teeth.

"How tall are you? You're old? Do you like my sissy?" Toni drilled in her squeaky voice.

"Toni, please leave Zach alone."

"She's all right. Is this your sister and mother?" Zach put his hand out for my mom.

She quickly shook his hand and, just as fast, dropped it. "Yes, I'm Tatum's mother. So, how long have you been driving, Zach?" Mom joined me at my side.

"Please, Mother." I put my head down.

"Since last summer. My birthday is right after the school cutoff."

"Well, I think we better be on our way." I had to get Zach out of there before he changed his mind about taking me to the dance.

We were about to walk out the door when I thought of something. "Zach, do I need my purse?"

"Don't bring it for money. This is my treat tonight. But if you want it to hold anything else, go ahead."

"I think I'll leave it, but how 'bout you hold something for me?" I jogged to my room and came back holding out my Chapstick. He took it from me with a sideways grin. "Can you put that in your pocket for me?"

"Sure."

"Bye, Mom, see ya at midnight."

"Have fun, Tate, and be careful," my mom yelled after us.

In my driveway, behind my mom's car, was his '73 V-8 Camaro. It was in better shape than I'd expected; the dull black paint was just slightly banged up around the bottom. Zach walked me around to the passenger side and opened the door for me.

"Thanks."

He shut the door after I tucked my gown into the car. The back seat was a bit messy, and the car had a stale aroma of pot. Yep, looked like the party mobile.

Climbing into the driver's seat, he started the Camaro and smoothly pulled away. Even over the stale pot smell, I could tell he wore cologne, nice cologne. I was impressed.

We were at the corner of the street. "Your mom is still in the window, watching us," he said.

"Are you serious?" I jerked my head to the side mirror. Looking out, I realized how dark the windows were tinted.

"No, she's gone now. I can't see your house anymore."

"I'm so sorry. My mom clearly lacks tact. I knew

she'd give you a hard time."

"It wasn't all that bad." He took a quick glance at me. "You look beautiful, Tate. And you smell intoxicating."

I appreciated the compliment. I just wished he hadn't said how good I smelled. Hearing that made me think of Kyle, and the day he'd told me that . . .

"Well, thanks. You look very nice yourself." Like, so nice, I wanted to gawk at him.

Zach wore black slacks, a white button-down shirt, and a thin black tie. Everything looked brand new and extremely expensive.

"So, you're the oldest. I see. How old is the blonde who was hopping around me laughing?" he said, breaking the silence.

"Oh, that's Toni. She's six. She really seemed to like you. Anyway, did you bring the tickets?"

"Tate, I'm a big boy. I said I'm treating you tonight, and I meant from the moment I pick you up till I drop you back off."

"Oh, a big boy, are ya? Okay. So, are you taking me out to dinner, too? *Big boy?*"

He took a quick glance at me and then turned back to the road. "Tate, I'll take you wherever you wanna go. Your wish is my command."

"Wow, the parking area looks almost full already." I had to quickly change the subject.

Zach offered to drop me off at the doors, but I didn't want him to leave me alone. After he parked, he came around to open my door. Gathering my dress, I carefully stepped out of the car and let the gown drop over my feet. The swoosh it made was impressive. Zach was staring.

It had been a long time since I'd felt like a little

girl playing dress-up and loving her gown. It had been a long time since I'd loved anything about myself.

Then I realized where Zach was looking. He had a perfect view of my cleavage. The top of my dress fit so well that it seemed to mush my bosoms a tad, making them seem bigger. Thank god for Miracle Bras. He was smiling, so I supposed he approved. Hmmm . . . curious, I wasn't mad he was looking at me like that. When Kyle looked at me like that, I knew he would expect something more than just a peek—that was annoying. Not Zach, though. It was as if he wanted nothing more than to admire me. Jeez, I liked being with him.

As we walked toward the front, a million things were going through my head. Should I take Zach's arm? Or hand? I needed to calm myself down.

Stepping to the side, Zach held the door open for me. We proceeded through the foyer and into the hall to give the attendants our tickets. Smiling at the chaperones, we headed toward the music.

Suddenly, Zach grabbed my hand and led me in. I said nothing, waiting to see where he took me. He found an empty area on the far right side of the cafeteria, against the railing and brick wall.

"Is this okay for now? I figured we could just scope things out for a bit, then get a table and refreshments after your friends get here."

"Sure. I don't want anything right now anyway."

I watched all the students coming in and handing their tickets over to the chaperones.

I heard someone familiar calling my name.

"Tate. Tatum, over here."

Andi was entering with Tommy. She had the largest smile on her face and was waving her arm like a lunatic.

They made their way to us, and I hugged them both.

Andi was wearing a black spaghetti-strap dress with a satin cream-colored ribbon under the bust. Her boobs looked great in that dress. It made me slightly jealous. Okay, screw "slightly," I was totally jealous. My poor padded bra was doing the best it could, but next to Andi, it wasn't worth the money I'd spent.

I needed to stand next to someone else. Where was Christy?

Zach leaned down to my ear and whispered, "You're perfect." He softly kissed the side of my head.

That was embarrassing. Did he notice me react to Andi's body? I turned to him and sighed, "Thank you." And then my mind immediately recalled my conversation with Val the night I slept over her house.

Past Andi, I saw Christy and a redhead coming in through the doors. I imitated Andi's obnoxious wave to get Christy's attention. Christy had on the dress I'd lent her, the one I'd worn to the Sweetheart Dance. She gave me a hug as Andi and Tommy scooted over to lean against the rail.

Christy squared off in front of me, eyeing my dress. "Tate, this is Ben. Ben, this is Tate."

I put my hand out. "Nice to finally meet you, Ben. I've heard so much about you."

"Nice to finally meet Christy's best friend . . ."

Best friend? Is that what Christy says about us, best friends? Interesting.

"Tate, maybe we should get a table on the other side of the rail. It's starting to fill up," Zach said.

We turned to walk around to the steps. But then

Zach swiftly hurdled the rail. He landed on the cafeteria floor and turned to face me with a huge smile on his face. I quickly picked my jaw up and narrowed my eyes. With his mouth twisted and eyes relaxed, he extended his right arm out to me.

"I don't think so. You're crazy if you think I'm jumping that." I started to walk away.

"Tatum, come here."

I shook my head no. Did he want to see me facedown on the floor?

"Tatum."

"What?"

"Turn your back to me."

I giggled a little.

"Just put your butt on the rail and hold the dress."

Following orders, I grabbed the bottom of my dress at my knees and wadded it close to my legs. *Dear lord. Why am I doing this? He's crazy. Why am I trusting him?* But I did.

"Now fall back, I have you."

"If you drop me, I'll kill you." Then I fell back into his arms.

And just like that, he was carrying me over to our table. I looked down and shoved the top of my body comfortably back down into my dress where it belonged. Zach glanced and looked back up again with a sideways smile.

"What in the world was the purpose of that, Zach?"

"Isn't it obvious?"

"If it were, would I be asking you?"

He looked in my eyes. "Look how close we are right now."

I immediately struggled to get down. Zach put me down at the table I'd originally picked. "We made a deal. We came together as friends."

Then I heard the rest of our group show up behind me. Zach stepped up to me and positioned his legs, slightly straddling my dress.

He grabbed the sides of my arms and whispered, "But we may leave as more."

CHAPTER 19

"*Zach.*"

"Tate, oh my gosh! You're crazy for jumping that rail in your dress." Christy exclaimed.

I gave Zach one last look before turning around to our company and plastering a fake smile on my face. "Oh, yeah, you know me. The wild and crazy one."

Suddenly it felt like we were being watched. I was afraid to look, and something was telling me not to. I glanced at my toes.

Just then, Zach bent down to the side of my face. "Yes, he's here. Don't look now. He's not happy to see us together."

I couldn't help it. I started to turn my head, but Zach stopped me by kissing my cheek.

He mumbled against my skin, "Stop." He backed away. "I told you not to look. Why ruin your night like that? Hell, why ruin my night? I really don't feel like getting my clothes dirty with scum."

Our faces were a few short inches from each other. He was grinning. If Zach was handsome before he smiled, he was gorgeous when he flashed those pearly whites.

Zach, Tommy, and Ben took off to get drinks for everyone. My girlfriends and I chose three seats facing outward toward the dance floor. They each took a seat beside me.

"Tatum, don't let that crazy nut job ruin your night. Zach is so sweet, and he's such a strong guy. He wouldn't let anything happen to you," Christy said.

"Oh, I'm not worried about that. I just don't want Asshole Football Player to try anything, for Zach's sake."

Andi's back straightened, then she grabbed my hand. "You're not going to believe who he brought to the dance."

I looked where she was facing. Kyle and Bonnie were walking out to the dance floor, holding hands. I felt like someone had hit me hard in the gut, knocking the air out of me. My body tensed, feeling my blood boil inside.

Both assholes, they were perfect for each other. "I'm glad it's over."

Christy and Andi shook their heads, agreeing with me.

Bonnie wore a horrific teal dress with poufy sleeves. I couldn't understand why Kyle paraded her around.

"So, you're glad what's over?" Zach said, placing drinks on the table.

Tommy and Ben followed him.

"Did you see who the Star Asshole brought in?" I asked in return.

"Yeah, Bonnie. You're not mad?"

"No, I feel disgusted, actually. Good riddance."

"Great. Let's dance, then." Zach put his hand out

for me.

"Really? You want to dance? Like, right now?"

He nodded.

"All right then, let's hit it." I took a quick sip of my iced tea and bolted out of my seat. I didn't waste any time.

Tommy and Andi joined us.

Thank god it was a slow song. My new shoes were the worst purchase so far. They already had my feet barking.

Slowing us down to half the beat, Zach pulled me into his body. "Did I tell you how wonderful you look tonight?"

"Yes, you did. At my house."

I decided to put some distance between our slow-dancing bodies and let him talk.

"That dress looks like it was made for you. It's actually not what I pictured you'd wear, but you look stunning in it. Tatum, I wish I didn't have to pretend any longer."

All of a sudden, he stopped dancing. With his head cocked, he leaned in for a kiss.

"Umm. I'm not sure this is the place." I crinkled my nose, being ashamed I couldn't come up with a cleverer excuse why not to kiss him there.

Zach stopped and stared at me. It was making me a little uneasy.

"Anything that happens tonight, Tatum, I swear, I won't take it in a way that would mean our friendship has led into a relationship. A kiss is innocent. Besides, I'm not that bad a kisser, am I?"

"I think my idea of innocent fun is different from yours," I replied, chuckling. I could feel my eyebrows rising. Zach was a great kisser. The sad fact was that I didn't trust myself.

I glanced back up at him and could see that he was clearly losing hope. This was sad, sad, sad. A tall, strong Italian sulking because he couldn't get a kiss. My lord. "Fine. Just friends having an innocent kiss—but I mean *just* as friends—" Before I could say anything more, he laid a good one on me.

Ten seconds or so later, a chaperone came by and cleared her throat. We quickly separated and ashamedly peered at the unknown parent.

"Okay, you two, maybe you should go have a seat for a while—and Mr. Bertano, no more slow songs for you." With that, she turned and continued her duty.

"How did she know my last name?"

Ducking my head down, I said, "I have no clue, but let's go sit back down for now. This is soooo embarrassing."

Zach took my hand. When we got to the table, everyone started to laugh.

"What? What's so funny?" I demanded an answer, stomping my foot.

I knew why they were laughing. So why couldn't they say it? I looked over at Zach, but he was looking at me like Bashful from *Snow White and the Seven Dwarfs* would. He was so cute.

"Oh. I get it. You think the chaperone scolded us. Well, ha, ha, ha, not likely."

I took my seat, keeping my head held high. My friends only thought that was funnier. Zach didn't offer any words of comfort. He sat there having what looked like a good quiet laugh to himself, avoiding my gaze. No clue why he was laughing. He was the one who couldn't dance to any more slow songs.

"So, did she forbid you to dance a fast song, too, Tatum?" Tommy teased.

"Oh, shut it. You're not funny, and how did you beat us back to the table?"

"Um, Tate, the song ended a while ago," Andi said.

Damn it.

꩜꩜꩜

It was nine o'clock or so, and my stomach wouldn't stop rumbling. I hadn't eaten a full meal since breakfast.

Zach leaned over to my ear. He whispered, "Do you wanna get dinner soon? I'm not rushing you."

"That'd be nice, thanks."

Just then, the song "Girls Just Want to Have Fun" by Cyndi Lauper came on. "Shall we?" I asked my girlfriends. "Zach and I are leaving after this."

In unison Christy and Andi said, "We shall."

We walked onto the dance floor and kicked off our shoes. I lifted up my princess dress and danced just like Cyndi had in her video. My dress sparkled perfectly under the disco ball. Andi and Christy both commented on it while we danced. I took it all in. Dancing under the disco ball, the dim lights, the sparkling from my body. I stared up at the ball and spun, having the time of my life. It had been a long time since I last felt this happy. After the song finished, we put our shoes back on and walked off the dance floor, holding each other's hands. It was a perfect song to end the night on.

But then I looked up, trying to maneuver us away from the crowd, and he stood in front of me. I jerked backward.

"What's wrong?" Andi asked. Then she noticed

who was in front of me.

Kyle and Bonnie had situated themselves in our path. I tried to casually look around them to find Zach. He was nowhere in sight. With us standing in the middle of such a thick crowd, I doubted he could see us. And Kyle had to know that.

The three of us held each other's hands, giving a bit of a squeeze for support.

"Wearing all white, Tate? Just curious . . . are you trying to look like a virgin tonight?" Kyle spat.

Christy gasped. Andi tried to lunge forward. I squeezed their hands, saying *please don't respond to him*. I smiled from ear to ear, grinding my teeth. Andi and Christy coughed; maybe I was squeezing their hands too tightly.

Kyle's eyes narrowed, focused on me. "What? You didn't tell your friends what you did and what you're doing?"

I definitely wanted him dead and now. Bonnie let out a wicked laugh. Behind my smile, I was confused. Why would she be happy that he raped me? Of course he wouldn't tell anyone that. What did he tell her?

"What is he talking about?" Christy whispered.

I squeezed even harder. Crap. I didn't know what he was talking about.

"All right, stop, you're breaking my hand. Damn," Christy quietly mumbled.

I eased my grip, and took a quick glance at Andi. Her cheeks were turning red, and I realized if I let go of her she would immediately attack Bonnie.

"So, you go from one guy to the next without letting your legs come back together . . . that's the game you're playing?"

A calm, strong voice came from behind Kyle and

Bonnie. "Tate's not playing any games, especially with you."

Tommy and Ben stepped around Kyle and Bonnie and took hold of their dates. Andi and Chris both were giving me sympathetic looks while they were being pulled away. I was left standing there alone.

Bonnie and Kyle looked over their shoulders, separated, and stepped back, appearing stunned. For a moment it was reminiscent of Moses parting the Red Sea.

Zach smiled, stepped between them, and put his right hand out for me. A big, sincere smile adorned his handsome face. I could have jumped him and given him the wildest kiss—if we were alone. Instead, I took my knight's hand.

Kyle looked like he was going to plow my date over any second.

Two weeks earlier, I would have passed out from fear at the sight of Kyle. But with Zach there, taking my hand, it was as if the past five months with Kyle were erased. Nearly.

Zach and I stepped right past as if nothing was more natural. Obviously that wasn't good enough, though, because Zach swiftly picked me up and cradled me to his chest.

I grabbed his face and turned it toward me. "Thanks." My eyes examined him. So tan . . . beautiful black eyebrows . . . a cute nose . . . and, god help me . . . those kissable lips.

He leaned down and gave me a quick peck on the cheek. In his arms, I felt perfect.

At the table, Andi and Christy were still in shock. Andi stood up when Zach put me down, and said, "Tate, bathroom."

It wasn't a question.

The three of us turned the corner for the girls' restroom and went inside. Andi quickly checked the stalls to see if we were alone.

There was no way in hell I'd let them interrogate me about what Asshole had said. So before either one of them said a word, I said, "He's fucking mental. I have no clue what's he's talking about." I turned around to face them, leaning against the sink. "Let it go. Who cares what he says. You know he's pissed because I never . . . you know . . . with him, that's all. He'll do anything to get a reaction."

Christy stood there with her arms crossed. "Well, that's clear. I mean, it's really none of anyone's business, and I don't care what he says anyway. As long as that's what you want."

"It absolutely is. Thank you."

Christy looked at Andi and sighed.

"Well, you know I wanna kill Bonnie. That girl has some nerve," Andi blurted out.

"I know she does, but I just ignore them."

"Well, you're doing a damn good job of it." Andi sniffed.

"I'm starving, and I think I've made myself the center of attention enough for one night. Can we go now? There's nothing else to talk about." I ended the conversation.

We got back to the table and Zach stood up.

Andi leaned into me. "He's so sweet."

"Are you ready to get dinner?" Zach asked.

"Yeah, I'm starving. And my feet are killing me."

We girls hugged each other goodbye, and then, without warning, Zach scooped me off my feet and away we went. My dress cascaded down his arms, and I thought to myself how pretty it was. I turned back one last time toward my girlfriends, and of course they were laughing with each other, waving to me.

We made our way around the cafeteria, this time taking the main hall.

That's when I noticed Tyler and two other guys, another blond guy and one who was insanely tall.

Tyler had a slender, Italian-looking girl hanging on his arm. S. Ne was gorgeous.

The blond guy laughed and flirted with his own date.

The insanely tall guy, monstrous in size, appeared to be alone. His gaze was unsettling.

Zach turned his head toward them and nodded.

The guys nodded in return. Nothing more.

"Who's that with Tyler?" I asked.

Zach gave my forehead a soft kiss, and said "My family."

I half-heartedly waved to Tyler. I never knew they were actually related. He nodded to me, but didn't wave back. The Italian girl looked at me while speaking to Tyler. They both stared at us and he agreed with whatever she had asked him. I felt like they were looking right through me.

Then the blond guy must have caught something they said because he then snapped his head to us.

That's when their attire caught my attention. They wore exactly the same as Zach: white, wrinkle-free, pressed shirts, thin, shiny, black ties, expensive, perfect-fitting black trousers. Feeling uncomfortable, I tucked my head against Zach's chest to hide my face.

Zach opened the front foyer door with his backside

and carefully maneuvered me outside. A brush of cool wind caught my shoulders. He must have noticed my shiver because he quickly darted for the car. My arms went around his neck to hang on.

Chuckling, I said, "Zach . . . don't drop me."

In that quick jog to his car, I became aware of the relaxed state I was in. It was nice.

Beside his car, he carefully put me down and reached in his pocket for his keys. He placed them on the rooftop instead of opening the door, and I looked up at him. He grabbed me around the waist and pushed my back up against the car.

I was looking up at him in shock. "What are—"

He cupped my face, and his lips pressed hard against mine. Oh, Jesus. Here it was, just what I was afraid of. Why couldn't I just enjoy this? I needed to kiss him and not worry, since no one was watching us for a change. I did want these lips. So nice, so soft, and they wanted me.

Zach moved his body up against mine. His lips traveled to my jawline and down my neck. I slipped my arms around his waist and cradled him close to me.

Oh god. He was perfect.

Zach took his hands down to my bare shoulders and gently massaged them. Instantly my body loosened up, becoming putty in his hands. I held my head back slightly and focused on breathing.

What was going on with me? His lips softly nibbled and nuzzled their way down my jawline, then my neck, working their way across my collarbone. I lifted my chin to give him better access, and he continued to the other side of my neck. I'd never felt this before, but somehow it felt like I'd done this a million times before with him.

Zach placed his hands under my armpits and picked me up. My backside pressed against his car. He was strong, real strong.

Jesus . . . he was driving me insane. Without thinking, I grabbed my dress and lifted it a bit to wrap my legs around him, squeezing my legs around his fit waist.

Kissing the side of my face, he said, "Oh, god. Tatum . . . ."

He took off, exploring my torso. To my surprise, I wanted to feel him, discover him.

Taking my hands to play with his hair, then the softness of his ears, then the side of his head—he was lovely. I was breathing so heavily, my chest was pumping, not able to take the tingling he was creating. The tingling feeling increased. The outdoor temperature increased fifty degrees or more. The warmth whirlwind around us moved faster than a tornado, pushing us closer.

That's when I felt how excited he was.

Oh Jesus . . . not that. No. No. No. This is going way too far. Don't think; just react before it's too late. Now. I placed my hands on his shoulders. "Zach." He froze. "It has to stop there." I took deep breaths, slightly pushing him.

"Tate?"

I didn't want to look at those eyes. I had to plant my feet. "Damn it. I'm letting this go too far." *I'm not thinking straight. You're too damn sexy for me to handle.*

"I'm not forcing you, am I?"

I slid down and looked him right in his eyes. "No. You're not." I exhaled and glanced farther away.

"God knows you feel great, but this scares me." I faced him. "I'm afraid that I'll lose you. The more we experiment, the more complicated it'll get in the future. Whatever this is, it's going way too fast, Zach."

"You won't lose me. Just let what's going to happen, happen."

I chuckled. "Oh, that's original. You say that now, but what about a month or five months from now? Are you going to say, 'Let's just be friends' and mean it? That's not how it works, and you know it. I really like being friends with you. I don't ever want to lose that, Zach. I've never heard of anyone being more than what we are and remaining friends afterward." I stepped away from the door.

Look at me and my first boyfriend, definitely not friends. And stupid me thought maybe we could be. Huh. I'm such a moron.

Zach looked at me with such heartbreaking eyes. At last he unlocked the door and opened it for me. I sat down and grabbed my dress to make sure it was all tucked in. I gazed up at him, letting him know he could shut the door.

"That dress shows your assets off too much." He swung the door closed with a thud.

He dropped in his seat and started the engine. I gawked at him in the aftermath of what he'd said.

Reaching in the back seat, he tossed me a black hooded sweatshirt. I'd never seen him wear it before.

"Do me a favor—cover yourself for a little while, please?"

"Of course, but why did you say that? That was really mean."

He focused on the steering wheel although he

spoke. "Tatum, if we can't go any further, it's best if I not see one curve of your body for a few minutes. I can't express how difficult it is for me to be in this situation with you." He turned to me. "I've wanted you for three years now, three years . . . and here I am. You look to die for, you're wonderful as a friend, and my feelings for you have only increased. I can't bear to look at you without responding. I don't want to lose you either—ever. We're perfect for each other and you know it. But mostly, I want to respect you and your decision to take this at your pace."

Zach turned back to the wheel. I mulled that over for a few minutes. He'd just spilled his guts to me. My heart sank as I did what he requested. He didn't look at me, not even a quick glance. The situation became too serious and tense; I didn't want to ruin the night. We'd been laughing and having fun. "Soo . . . are you saying that since my legs are completely covered by my dress that they're not one of my better assets?"

I looked at Zach with a smile. Waiting for his response, waiting for him to blow it off and laugh with me. I considered myself clever at that moment.

"You tease." He rolled his head to me and chuckled, "Really?" He squared off at me in his seat. "Let me tell you something, hon—"

My back straightened, and my eyes couldn't open any wider.

"No matter what . . . I'm a guy that's shutting down something strong right now. Tatum, it's not fair to tease me." His chin was down and his eyes serious.

I swallowed . . . hard. He went back to driving away, and just like that, my smile melted away with embarrassment.

I didn't even think of it that way. Me, a tease? Well, shit. That backfired.

CHAPTER 20

I didn't say a word until Zach asked me about restaurants for dinner.

"I'm so hungry, I don't care at this point," I replied.

"How about Casa Gallardo? And don't forget, I'm buying."

"Well, then, make it Tony's, downtown." We looked at each other and chuckled. "Casa is perfect, thanks." I wouldn't do that to Zach—make him take me to the most expensive restaurant in St. Louis. Not yet, anyway.

"Zach, I'm sorry if I teased you. I didn't see it that way, but I can see how you do."

He glanced over at me with a gentle grin. "Forget about it. No harm done."

It was quiet in the car again until Zach switched on his tape player. An awful screeching sound erupted from the speakers.

"Oh my god, what is that?" I shouted, covering my ears.

"Sorry." He turned it down. "So you don't like the new Anthrax album?"

"That's actually considered music?"

He laughed. "I'll take that as a no. Do you want

me to turn it off?"

"Well, no, it's okay. How about just turn it down? Like, real low?" I looked over at him and he was grinning as he turned it all the way down.

Once we parked, he helped me with my door and took my hand. The gentlemanly behavior continued as Zach opened the restaurant's door for me and stepped around my dress to tell the hostess, "Party of two." When he did, Zach looked back at me and couldn't have looked happier.

Over dinner, we had great conversation, laughed, and ate. Not rushing. We had such a wonderful time that I did what I could to extend my evening out with him. He did exactly what he'd promised, he treated me.

When we were pulling away from the restaurant, he asked, "So, what would you like to do for an hour? We could drive around for a bit and then I could take you home. Or we could go back to my place, it's quiet."

Remember what he did in the parking lot? Imagine what he'd do in the privacy of his home . . . yikes. "Zach Bertano, I don't think so."

"All right, we'll just drive for a bit, and then I'll take you home."

"Sounds good to me. But you know, if you don't want to, you can just take me home early. I won't be offended."

Zach looked over at me. "Tate, I want to spend every waking moment with you. I wish you didn't have a curfew at all."

"Uh, don't you have a curfew?"

"No, my parents are probably out partying with my uncles. Are you sure you don't wanna come back to my house?"

"I'm not sure that's such a good idea, but thanks for offering. I need to make sure I'm home by midnight or my mom will kill me. I can guarantee she's still up waiting to make sure I'm in that door at the stroke of twelve."

"That's crazy."

"Well, that's my mom and I don't want myself grounded from you." Dang it, I didn't mean to say that.

Zach pulled into a local park, St. Ferdinand.

"What are we doing here?" I breathed, trying to hide my nervousness.

He parked under a tree. Cut the engine. Then turned the music to just audible.

He unbuckled himself and turned toward me. "I thought we could talk a bit."

Oh. Talk, okay. He's so easygoing. I love it. "Sure, what's on your mind?" *You idiot . . . look at his face. You know what he's thinking. Quick, think faster.* "Did you enjoy the dance?" *Yeah, yeah. That sounds good. Nothing sexual. Mind off of sex.*

"I did. How about you? No one ruined it for you?"

"Nope." I looked at him with a grin. "Thanks to you." Jesus, I was a moron. *Great, now look at his face.* His eyes were starting to droop. He was moving in. "It was nice of you to take me out tonight." Yep, I was rattling on, as boring as could be.

"No problem. I wanted to." He glanced away, then back at me. "Tate, would you like to smoke with me?"

"Smoke? I don't smoke. And I didn't realize you did, either." That had taken an ugly turn. Maybe we should just make out. "Do you mind if I do?"

"No, that's okay. Just roll down the window, or my mom will smell it on me."

He rolled his window down and moved things around and got things out.

He stopped and turned at me. "It's not a big deal to me. I don't need to if you're not going to join me."

"I said it's all right. Go ahead, Zach."

"Why don't you? You know . . . smoke? Just curious."

He lit up and started sucking in.

My mouth dropped open. Shit. I knew it.

"Tate, are you okay?"

"It's pot?"

"Yeah, what did you think I was talking . . . oh wait, you thought cigarettes?"

"Yes, cigarettes."

One side of Zach's mouth turned up in a grin. He rolled the window down a bit more and turned toward the crack in the window.

I wonder if his parents have ever smelled it on him? I don't like this, not one bit. Why does he have to smoke? Do a lot of boys smoke? I'm sure my girlfriends don't smoke. Dang it, the longer he smokes the more pissed I'm getting. Well, don't I sound like Miss Goody Two-Shoes of the year? Ugh. He's been sucking away for a while, that should be enough, right?

"Well, I should get home soon." I looked at him. Zach looked tired. "Are you okay? Can you drive?"

Zach reached his free arm around me and put his head on my shoulder.

Yep, that was enough. *This is just great. My date is gone, and I need to be home in thirty minutes.* "You need to sober up in twenty-five minutes, or I may have to throw your butt in the back seat. I can't be late."

Zach started laughing at me.

"What's so funny?"

"Nothing, you're just so damn cute, Tate."

"Oh, well, I'm glad you're having a good time."

Zach fiddled around with his tapes and put something different in. "Here, this is for you. Listen, honey."

I couldn't help but roll my eyes. *Great, he's fricking high. This sucks.*

It was "All of My Love" by Led Zeppelin. *Well, shit, just shoot me now.* "Zach, please, why are you doing this?"

"I've told you before I've loved you since the seventh grade. You're the girl I fantasize about."

Okay, I was just going to ignore that he admitted he fantasized about me, because I knew damn well what kind of fantasies those were. "Yes, yes, I know. Will you please stop saying that? And correction, my dear," I said, putting my right index finger up. "You told me you'd *liked* me since the seventh grade." I flung myself back in my seat and exhaled loudly, becoming more tired by the moment.

"Tate, come here." Zach reached for me.

"No, leave me alone. You just ruined a perfectly good evening."

He looked over at me with the most ridiculous smirk. What a hormonal idiot.

"You know how good we would be together?"

"Oh, well, if this is a sneak peek, you're right, Zach. It would be just perfect."

He laughed while gently tapping my leg.

"Cut it out." I took his hand off my thigh and

flipped it to his side of the car. "You have about another twenty minutes to sober up." I stared back out the window. I couldn't believe he was high. And here I was sitting like a fricking bump on a log. We'd been having a good time. Why did he have to ruin everything? Grrrrr.

About ten minutes went by without either one of us talking.

"Zach, I need to be home in fifteen. Are you going to be okay in ten?"

His head rested against the seat. He rolled it toward me. "Yeah, I'll be fine. I can take you right now if you want."

"No, I wanna make sure you're better. We're not going to cause an accident." It would be interesting to see how much he remembered after he woke up the next day. "You know, I enjoy your company and friendship, but under sober circumstances. Tonight proves that we have different interests. I want you to respect that of me. As much as you think we would be good together, I'm sure the more time you spend with me, the more you'll see it wouldn't work. This opened my eyes. I like you a lot, and I care so much for you, but I can't say I love you."

He was so quiet I thought he might have fallen asleep.

"Zach, are you okay?"

I finally saw him smile at me. "I hear you. It's fine that you're not in love with me. I'll take whatever relationship I can get. Who knows? I might even grow on you." He leaned forward, getting extremely close to my face. I watched his every move.

He put his hand on the side of my head and cradled it, softly. "I do understand—and respect that.

It's one of the many things I love about you. You're so pure. You're honest and straightforward, and, of course, beautiful. I'll take you home now," he said.

He dropped his hand and started the engine. I exhaled.

Zach glanced at me. "Are you okay? Why don't you sit back and buckle so we can go?"

I sat back. Looking out the window, I thought about how he saw me. "Pure"? That hit me like a ton of bricks. If only he knew.

⁕⁕⁕

We pulled up in front of my house, and I could tell he was very sleepy.

"Zach, how about I run in the house, tell my mom I'm home, and see if it's okay if I sit out here for a while. I'll grab ya a Mountain Dew and see if it makes a difference. I don't want you to have to drive home by yourself like this."

He pulled up the hand brake and leaned over to me. "Are ya worried about me?" He wore that stupid grin on his face. "Ahhh, that's sweet."

I surprised myself by popping him on the cheek. "Yeah, ya jerk, and you're not going to do this to me again."

"Ow," he said, putting his hand on his cheek.

Shit. I shouldn't have hit him. *Please don't come after me, please. I didn't mean that.*

Holding his cheek, he glared at me.

I sat against the door. My head was turned to the side with my eyes squinted closed, desperately hanging onto the door handle. I held my breath, praying he didn't strike back.

"Tatum?"

I barely peeked at him.

His head bopped. "It's all right. I'm not glad you hit me, but I would never touch you. Go inside and ask your mother for more time." He nodded his head at me, lowering his hand from his cheek. "It's all right, hon."

I jumped out of the car and ran up to the house. I went inside and quickly closed the door behind me. Putting my back to the door, I took a few quick breaths. I was stupid to hit him. Why had I done that?

"Mom, it's me. I'm home," I loudly whispered down the staircase.

"Oh, okay, Tate. Make sure you lock the door." Voila, she was lying in bed, waiting.

"Um, well, I was wondering if it would be okay for me to sit out in front with Zach to talk a bit longer?"

"You have twenty minutes. That's it. No more tonight."

"Thanks, Mom." I ran to get a thick sweater from my room and a cold Dew on my way back out. I jumped in the car and told him I had twenty minutes. He was looking even more tired.

"Here, drink this."

He took it and popped it open. I sat back in my seat. "I wish you didn't do that."

"Do what?" He gulped.

I gave him the evil eye. "Why do you have to smoke pot?"

"Not sure." He looked away for a moment before glancing back at me. "It's always been around me. I guess that's why."

"How? Don't your parents care, or know?" Why was he smiling at me?

"My parents know. Mom doesn't mind as long as

it's not much."

I blocked his voice out of my head. Holy shit, his parents didn't care? My god, my mother would send me to rehab and tell everyone that I went to an all-girls school out-of-state for a better education. Clearly, we came from different backgrounds.

"So, I take it your parents would hate it if you did?" he asked.Maybe the pot made him think he was funny. "Um, yeah. My parents would mind. I'd be grounded forever."

"Oh." He turned away.

Zach had almost the whole soda down in about five minutes and let out a loud belch.

"Ugh, you're such a jerk."

"Oh, am I? Didn't you tell me to down a Mountain Dew? Jeez, Tate, if I'm a jerk for doing what you told me, what does that make Kyle?"

Stab wound to the heart.

I jab-punched him in the shoulder. Evidently, he was sobering, since he caught my wrist before I could get back to my seat. We froze, staring at each other. He reached down and reclined his seat, and we went flying into the back of his car. With one strong pull, I was on top of him. I looked up at him with horror on my face. Zach took control.

The reality: if Zach really wanted to have his way with me, he could.

He grabbed my waist and pulled me up on him. He leaned forward and kissed me.

"Zach, stop it," I mumbled between his lips.

He backed his face away, but kept his firm grip around my body. "Honey, let it go."

"You're acting just like *him*—an insensitive jerk. This is the last time I'm going anywhere with you."

Saying I'd never go anywhere affected me more than I imagined. There was immediate regret.

"Look at me."

I did. "What?"

He spoke softly. "I'm not him."

"I know you're not. I'm sorry. That was a low blow," I replied. I was so confused. Did I want him or not?

"I'm sorry, but you know how long I've been interested in you, honey." He examined every feature on my face with a grin.

"Why haven't you ever told me before?" "I've asked you to do things with me and you always turned me down. I didn't want to get rejected anymore."

He asked me to do things as a group. I guess that was his way of testing the waters before he asked the bigger question: would I go on a date with him? But I hadn't because of being with others. If it had been just with him, I would have.

"Tell me you don't feel something for me, Tate. Tell me if you don't."

I couldn't look at his face, even though I was about to tell the truth. "I do feel something. Now, what that something is, I don't know."

I turned my head up to his. Our eyes met. Could I live with his habit? Gosh, he was so handsome, I'd forgive a lot. Look at those eyes, so dark. That was all it took, those eyes. He was moving in and watching me. I chuckled. He was afraid that I would reject his kiss. Not a chance, not now. I took my lips to meet his, and the instant our lips touched, that sensation zinged from my lips to my toes. Instant turn-on.

His left hand wandered down too far on my

backside, so I promptly moved it to a comfortable height. He chuckled under my lips and put his warm hands under the back of my sweater. For a split second, I could feel the old wounds on my back. But his hands were like warm silk sheets draping around my bare skin. That was my undoing.

Caress. Squeeze. Release. Repeat.

Zach's hands were so warm and excited—moving with the right amount of tension and slowness. His right hand started unzipping my dress. And, just like I'd feared, I wasn't stopping him. He was making me feel too good to stop there. He pulled it down a few inches so that it was loose on the top and sagging open. Still kissing me, he began stripping my sweater off my shoulders. He backed away from my face and took that moment to examine my cleavage. I felt like straddling him, so I did. Zach gasped to God. Then he kissed me again in a hurry, wrapping his torso around mine, encasing me.

We had to stop. This was insane. Then I noticed the thing that scared me the most, feeling how I affected him. I sighed, shaking my head. I could control myself and stop if need be, but could he? This was totally pushing it with him. I wasn't going to do what he wanted.

I pushed myself off of him and dove for my seat.

"I think you sobered up enough to make it home safely now." Right, who was I kidding? Like that had been the only reason for him to stay.

I straightened the skirt part of my dress. Zach had pushed it up more than I had realized. I wasn't about to call attention to my unzipped dress. I wasn't able to reach the back, but it would be stupid to ask him to help.

Zach gently stroked my cheek. "I'll call you tomorrow. Goodnight, hon."

He couldn't be serious. It was a little shocking that he was letting me go.

"But, Tate, pull your dress up before I lose it," he said, admiring me.

I looked down and realized most of my lace bra was showing. Without another word, I closed my sweater over the sagging dress.

"Goodnight, and be careful." I stepped out of his car and ran up to my house, frantically shutting the door behind me.

Shit. I'd known I'd lose control with him.

CHAPTER 21

My family went out for breakfast the next morning, so I got to sleep in until the phone woke me up at eleven.

Clearing my throat and putting the receiver up to my ear, I said, "Hello?"

"Hey, it's Valerie."

"Oh, shit."

"Oh, no. Tell me you didn't do anything."

"I had a rough night, don't start. And no, I didn't do anything you wouldn't have done."

It sounded like she was choking on the other end. I laughed. "Are you okay?"

"What do you mean, you had a rough night? Did something happen?"

"What didn't happen?" I told Val everything from the moment Zach picked me up to him carrying me out to his car. She didn't interrupt once. Till—

"Do you like him?"

"You're not telling me what you think." I didn't really want to get into the topic of my feelings. My head was a mess at that point. I was honestly confused. It really upset me that he had smoked during our date. But then there was how relaxed he made me, as if we'd known each other our whole lives.

"Simple. I think he loves you, and I'm wondering if you subconsciously love him."

"Val, I've been over this a million times—I don't. Like I told him, it would never work. We don't have the same interests. Everything is just fun right now, and I want to keep it that way." Fun, yeah, everything with Zach was fun, really fun. But darn it, that fun was messing with my head too much, and all I wanted was more fun with him.

"Well, if you're sure, I think it's for the best. So, did you have a good time besides the Asshole Football Player thing?"

"I did, and I'll tell you what I really enjoyed. Seeing *his* face when Zach came to my rescue. No matter what, Zach won't back down from him." I thought it was time to change the subject. "So, what did you do last night? Did you go out with Scotty?"

Val filled me in on her night. Then it was time to inform her about the new job that I was being made to get. She was disappointed, too.

"What does that mean for our weekends?"

"Plain and simple, Val. I won't have many. I don't want to think about it right now."

⁓⁓⁓

Zach hadn't called like he'd said he would. I wondered if he was going to. So, when the phone did ring, I ran for it, thinking it was him.

"Tate, I have your new work schedule."

"Wonderful. How bad is it, Mom?"

"Oh, it's not too bad. You work Saturday and Sunday from eleven to eight at night."

"All day? Oh, man—" I flopped back on my bead.

"Well, it's your first weekend working, so of

course it's going to be more. I told them I don't want you working all day on Sundays as a regular routine."

"Thanks, but it's just my whole weekend—"

"Look, this is what it's like getting a job. You have a responsibility now. You need to start earning your own play money. We'll be home later. Get your homework done," Mom said.

"Fine." I slammed the phone down.

Ring.

Jesus, didn't I just hang up with her? Now what? I jerked the ringing phone back up. "Yeah?"

"Ehhhh... Tatum? It's Zach. Can you talk?"

"Sure." Great, now he calls. Why couldn't he call me before I spoke with my mom? It just kept getting better.

"Oh. Okay. Um, look about last night—"

"Just forget it. It's not a big deal."

"Are you sure? Because you sounded a little mad when you answered the —"

"Zach, I'm not mad at you. It's my mom. She just gave me my schedule for this new job she's making me get, and I have to work all next weekend. And, since you're asking, I really don't like that you smoke pot. Why can't there be a guy who's nice and doesn't do any drugs? I mean, is it too much to ask?" I heaved my chest, feeling the frustration that he wasn't the perfect guy. Why would I let his one fault ruin my weekend, though?

"I'm sorry about smoking, but I asked you to tell me if you'd prefer me not to. If you don't want me to, I won't."

"I know, but who wants to tell their date what to do? I don't. So just forget about it."

"Tatum, tell me if you'd like me to leave you

alone. I don't want to, but I will."

Oh, for Christ's sake. Now he was paranoid. "No, Zach. Not necessary. And to be honest"—I laughed—"I don't see you leaving me alone."

He chuckled with me. "You're right. You may have me for life."

※ ※ ※

Monday morning Christy and I caught up on the bus. I didn't tell her about the illegal stuff with Zach. I wasn't going to tell anyone. It was no one's business. Wrong or right, people make judgments, and there was no reason to lead anyone to wrongly judge him.

I got to my locker as usual and Andi was there, enthusiastically talking to Zach.

"Hey, guys." I said, taking my stuff out of my locker.

"Hey. I have to go, so I'll just see you two at lunch," Andi said, walking off.

I still hadn't said a word to Zach as we headed to our first hour. Second hour came, and we still hadn't said a word to each other.

Before I walked into my third hour, I called Zach to me, taking my back against the wall, off to the side of the door. He was hesitant and unsure of my intentions. He had been reading me loud and clear all day. I needed things to cool down a bit.

"Yes, Tate?" He put his left hand on the wall above my head. His typical power stance.

I turned to him and whispered, "I'm sorry for being so rude today. To be honest, I've been like this to avoid . . . I mean to avoid . . ." Shit, I couldn't say it. I couldn't say *avoid kissing you, feeling you, because this just won't work between us*. I reached up and kissed his cheek. "I'll see you after class." He put his hand where I'd kissed him. I walked into class, not waiting for him to respond further.

I sat in my usual seat up by Mr. Connor's desk and waited for him to start class.

Eric, who now always sat behind me, whispered, "Tate, Zach's at the door trying to get your attention."

I was caught off guard and looked up at the door. Kyle was for sure watching the whole thing from the back of the class. My eyes weren't the only ones watching this. The room got quiet.

"What?" I mouthed.

"I love you." He mouthed back.

I swallowed, hard. "Go to class before you're late." I nudged my head to go.

He loves me?

He nodded with an immense grin.

Huh?

Still wearing that grin, one side of his mouth went higher along with his eyebrows.

Look away. Look away. Out of the corner of my eye, I saw him take off. *Oh Jesus, now what do I do? So he loves me? Like he just said, "Tatum, I love you." Oh my gosh! He must have been serious. Kyle never told me that he loved me. Never. I never told him either, 'cause I didn't.*

"Did you two have fun this weekend?" Eric whispered.

I twisted backward; he was wearing a smart-alec smirk. "Um, I don't think that's any of your business, sweetheart."

"Uh huh, okay," Eric replied, teasingly. Then he rolled his tongue around on the inside of his mouth.

I went to pop him one, but he blocked me. "Oh,

can it, you buffoon."

I caught a glimpse of Kyle's face when I was spinning around again. He wasn't disturbed in his usual way. Something was different. No idea what that could mean, but sooner or later there would be something else to deal with, that I was sure of.

※※※

Most of the week went along as boring as could be. It was just what I wanted and needed.

Then, at lunch on Thursday, it all blew up in my face. And I'd been that close to having a good week at school.

Andi threw her books on the lunch table.

She was noticeably pissed off. "You're not going to believe what Football Player is going around saying now."

"Oh, Andi, I don't care what he's saying," I said, getting my wallet.

Zach looked up at her. "What's he saying?"

I stood up. "Well, since you need to get this off your chest, I'm gonna go get the food while you two chat. 'Cause I don't give a shit what he says."

Andi nodded and I walked off. I heard Zach's chair so I turned around.

He was holding money out. "Money?"

"I'll get it later."

I came back five minutes later to a quiet table even though they were both still there.

Taking in the tense atmosphere, I handed out the food and drinks. Andi thanked me, but Zach was silent. He just took his drink and gulped. Patting Zach's shoulder, I asked, "Hey, are you okay?"

He said nothing and kept his face tucked. Zach imitated a statue. Not moving, not even eating. Just simply holding his Pepsi can. No response.

I patted his arm again. "Zach? Hon?"

He was taking this statue thing too far. I couldn't see his eyes. He had his head tucked so far down I couldn't see his face.

This might be serious; he refused to respond to me.

I jerked my head toward Andi. "What did you say to him? Is this about Asshole?"

Andi shook her head with apprehensive eyes. "I just told him what K . . . I mean . . . yeah, what he's saying."

Some guys walked up to our table. Andi and I turned.

"Oh, hey, Tyler. How are you?" I asked.

The other two guys from the dance were there as well.

Zach didn't look up. Not even a flinch.

Tyler had eyes for one person—Zach. "I'm fine. But do you mind if I borrow Zach here for a minute?"

I shook my head.

The two other guys had slight grins on their faces.

The shorter one, who stood in the middle, was a beautiful version of a Californian blond surfer dude. He had striking blue eyes. I swallowed hard, somewhat intimidated by his beauty. Jesus, he was gorgeous.

The blond put his hand out to me. "Hi, I'm Bobby. Nice to finally meet you, Tatum."

"Thanks. Umm, nice to meet you," I replied, dropping my hand from his.

"And I'm Matt. Nice to finally meet Zach's Tatum." He too wanted to shake my hand.

Matt was much taller than any of the other boys at school. Hell, he was taller than most men for that matter. He had dark brown hair in long shaggy layers. I shook his hand. Damn. That was a strong grip.

And Zach still hadn't spoken or budged. Giving my attention back to Zach, I gently placed my hand on his shoulder again.

What in the world was going on with these guys? And what was wrong with Zach? Was it these guys? Why did they, or Tyler, want him? The worrying was making my gut feel nauseous.

"Man, we need to go." Tyler's voice was so cold I could feel a chill in the air.

Without warning, Zach crushed the Pepsi can in his hand. Andi and I jumped back, trying to avoid the spraying soda.

He got up and nonchalantly wiped his hand off. I didn't know what to do. Zach faced me. Misery was written all over his handsome face, and that was scary to me.

Zach held onto my shoulders while I desperately tried to read those black eyes as fast as I could.

He gently swiped a few spatters of soda off my face. "Tate, I may not be in class the rest of the day."

"Why? What's going on?"

He finally met my eyes. "Because I have something to do. I'll call ya."

"Sure, but—" My breath shook when I whispered, "Zach, you're scaring me. What's this about?"

His friends hadn't moved. Tyler and Matt stood there frozen, with an intensity about them that would give you the willies. Bobby stood there smiling at me, bouncing around like a child waiting to open presents.

"Nothing, Tatum. I just can't have anyone going around talking trash like that about us."

Before I could say another word, he pulled me

against his body and took my lips, fiercely kissing them. For once, his actions made sense to me. This was a goodbye kiss. It had to be. God knew I didn't want to let him go, no matter what this meant.

In hopes it wasn't a goodbye kiss, I gently placed my hands behind his head to pull him closer, tugging him to me, praying this would get him to stay.

He leaned back and whispered, "God. I love you. I'll talk to you soon." He bent down and gently gave my forehead a soft peck.

"No, don't go. I'm scared. Who cares what he says about us? I don't. Seriously, stay here with me." I then resorted to begging with my eyes.

Zach took a step back from me without another word. He grabbed his books and shot Andi a quick glance. "See ya, Andi."

Andi awkwardly waved goodbye. Zach turned back to me, holding his books down along his leg.

I whispered, "Please stay?"

He shook his head, then mumbled, "Don't worry about it. I love you."

Don't worry about it? And he kept telling me he loved me. This was getting out of control. Why wouldn't he just tell me what was going on? I mouthed, "I know you do." My nerves were shot. Vomiting would come soon.

Blink.

He casually walked away, the guys in tow.

Andi and I watched them walk up the steps. Bobby looked back at me and grinned with a half nod.

Was he talking to me?

Half nod again.

I tried to stop moving my head from side to side like a dog does, even though this was more confusing than a Rubik's Cube.

He smiled widely and turned away.

My life began moving in slow motion, starting with the four of them walking away.

Something was different, way different. It required me to look closer. Their aura was speaking to me. Zach led the way. Tyler and the rest of the pack followed, Matt pulling up the rear. I focused on Bobby. He was flexing his fists and then stretching them out, flexing and stretching.

Shit. Why would he be doing that?

Then they were gone.

Zach wasn't in our fourth hour.

When fifth hour came along, Kyle wasn't there either.

CHAPTER 22

The moment the last bell rang, I ran for my bus like an Olympian in the hundred-meter sprint. Zach had to be okay, he had to be.

Christy plopped down next to me on the bus. "Okay, so tell me what's going on."

I whipped my head at her. "Why? What did you hear?"

She wiggled her butt in the seat. "Just that Kyle, or Asshole, was spreading some pretty spicy rumors."

I swallowed. "What rumors?"

"Not sure, but something about how you and Zach," she looked around for prying ears and then leaned over to me, "got cozy after the dance. You'll have to tell me later." She winked.

In that instant, my blood pressure skyrocketed and my face contorted. Bastard.

"Oh, calm down. It could be worse. Now, are you going to tell me what's going on with Zach or not?"

Christy was the only one to ever dismiss my temper so easily, well, besides Val. "Nothing, but he left early. My gut is telling me that he and his friends have something to do with Asshole not being in fifth hour, too. I need to get home. I wish this fricking bus would take off already."

"Well, I hope he's okay."

"I do, too. Tyler and that Matt guy looked serious as a heart attack, almost scary. Except for Bobby."

"Wait. Who are those guys?"

Thank god the bus was finally rolling. "His friends, I guess. And Tyler's related to him."

"But the one guy wasn't serious looking?"

"Yeah, Bobby."

"Well, why didn't he scare you?"

If Chris only knew what this guy looked like. Ha, please, he didn't scare me. Reflecting on it . . . he sort of resembled Zach, but blond and a bit shorter. Great-looking guys, beautiful in different ways.

After an agonizing twenty-minute ride home, Christy and I were in her bedroom, sitting on her bed.

"I'm glad your parents let you come over. So, have you heard anything from Zach?"

"No, he's scaring the crap out of me. I've called his house and no one's answering. I made sure to leave a vague message, though. Ugh. What have I gotten myself into?" I flung my head back on her pillow and stared up at the ceiling. "I'm worried sick right now, and why?" I covered my face.

"Don't worry, Tate. He'll be okay. But you know, this is all Asshole's fault."

I turned to look at Christy. "You're right. Why can't he just leave me alone?"

"I don't know. But I have a feeling that Zach might be adding fuel to the fire."

"Brilliant. That's gotta be it. Asshole is feeding off of this."

"Oh, no, I just thought of something else." Christy tilted her head toward the ceiling.

"Yeah?"

Christy sat down and faced me. "What did you and Zach do after the dance?"

I sprung up like a daisy. "Oh no. I didn't even think of that. He must have followed us out to Zach's car . . . wait. Is he stalking me? And the moron came with Bonnie. What was she doing? Following me too? But it was dark."

I was already embarrassed by what we'd done in the parking lot; most girls might not have been, but I was. Thinking that someone actually watched us made bile come up my throat.

Christy cupped my hand in hers. "So you two—?"

"No, no. Absolutely not." I jerked my hand away.

"Then what did he see in the parking lot?"

Oh, well, shit, I thought we were alone. He saw too much, that's what he fricking saw.

"It's okay, Tate, I won't judge you for it. I've been meaning to tell you . . . I'm not one anymore, either. I haven't been for a while."

Christy wasn't a virgin? Who'd been her first then? "I think you're getting the wrong impression. I'm sorry you just spilled your business to me, but Zach and I didn't. I mean, yeah, we made out, but that's all."

"Wait." She slapped her leg. "You mean to tell me you two never loosened your clothes?"

"Exactly. Zach didn't even get to second base in the school parking lot."

Christy dropped her head. We were both embarrassed.

Her head popped up. "Did you hear a car?"

We bolted for her front door. Her phone rang, stopping us in our tracks.

Christy snatched the receiver. "Hello?" Her eyes enlarged. "Dear god, Zach, she's been worried sick about you. Yeah, yeah, here she is."

Without an invite, I grabbed the phone out of her hand. "Zach?" Hearing his breath was all it took to feel the day's events, making me weak at the knees. "Oh gosh, are you okay?"

"I'm at your house. Come home, Tate."

He didn't have to say it twice. I slammed the phone down and darted out Christy's door.

My heart pounded so hard it made it difficult to run down the street.

I hurdled the front steps with Christy right behind me. Then I twisted the doorknob. The front door was unlocked. Christy and I both stopped and stared at each other.

She took a step back, examining the door front. "Nothing seems broken into. How did he get inside? Aren't your parents out for dinner?"

"Yeah. I don't know how he got in, but my parents never leave the house unlocked."

We stepped inside. Silence. Zach was nowhere to be seen.

Christy and I stopped in the middle of the living room, looking around. "My bedroom?"

She nodded and we ran for the closed door.

Once my hand hit the doorknob, I realized how scary this could be. We slowly opened the door. Zach sat on the edge of my waterbed, appearing to be in deep thought.

The moment he noticed we were there, his head popped up. "Tate!"

I collapsed my head on his chest, relieved that he was in one piece. The stress came gushing out of me into his arms. "Oh Zach, you had me so worried. What's going on?" I asked, glancing up at his face. Something caught my attention on the corner of his lip. I stepped back. "Is that blood? What happened? Did you go looking for Asshole? You can't be that stupid."

Zach grinned. "Okay, I won't tell you what happened, then."

"No, tell me if you're hurt anywhere else besides that cut on the corner of your mouth. Did *he* do that?"

He wore pride across his face well. "Without all the gruesome details, I'm fine except for this on my mouth—a cheap shot—and I may get a few bruises, no big deal. So forget about it, that asshole could never hurt me."

"But what about your friends, Tyler and them? Were they with you?""Yeah, they had to be. They're fine, but if you're worried, Bobby broke his middle finger. And Tyler might have a broken nose. It's no big deal. You wanna hear about Asshole?"

Jesus Christ. This was crazy. I met Zach's eyes again. "I'm scared. I don't know how you guys are going to cover this up."

"We don't really have to. So do you want to know about Ass or would you rather wait till school on Monday to see what his injuries are? Besides, I'm not a hundred percent sure myself." Zach seemed more than confident of his performance.

"Oh jeez, Zach. Okay, I guess you better prepare me." I took a seat on my bed. Zach followed me on one side while Chris took my other.

Christy bent forward and said, "I hope you got him good, Zach. He deserves it."

I had to stop myself from elbowing her.

"Well, he's going to the hospital for a dislocated shoulder."

Christy and I gasped in unison, "The hospital?"

"Yeah, I offered to pop it back in place, but he wanted to go to the hospital." Zach rolled his eyes as if he popped dislocated shoulders back in all the time, no big deal.

"Good, maybe it will be worse," Christy popped off.

"Don't say that. Zach can get in trouble." "I won't. It's covered. And no one will tell the whole truth. They know better."

Without thinking, my hand went to Zach's leg. "Who did he have with him? Anybody? I mean, you guys didn't gang up on him, four to one, did you?"

"Of course not, do you think that weasel would go to a fight alone? No, he had three other guys with him—we each took one. I, of course, took Asshole. Man . . . I'd been waiting for months to get a piece of that guy." Zach shook his head before turning back to me. "Strutting around like he's sooo cool. And the whole time you dated him, he told every guy in school about you. I mean, private shit about you, Tate. He won't now, though."

I was shocked. No, I was sick. That bastard.

Zach mushed his lips against my forehead, and kissed me. "Trust me, everything he got, he deserved. I promise."

Mother Mary and Joseph. "I think that's all I want to hear. I don't understand why you couldn't let it go."

He sighed, clearly apprehensive about saying something. "Well, I had to do it. Forget what shit he said about you when you were dating the ass, but what he said about us? I'll be damned if I'll sit there and do nothing. That's all you need to know. Don't worry about it."

Christy started to rub my shoulder. Anger brewed fast. *"Don't worry about it?"* Was he insane? You didn't send someone to the hospital without getting in trouble with the law. "Why couldn't you just let it go, Zach? Who cares? I don't care what he's saying about me or what anyone else thinks about me. You did exactly what he wanted. You just added fuel to the fire."

The features on his face hardened. "Because I had to. I can't say why, just that I had to. That's all you need to know."

I leaped to my feet. "Oh, really?" I raised my voice at him. "Well, that's a bunch of shit. Fighting him is the last thing I want anyone to do *because of me*." I started pacing in circles; it took everything I had to not start kicking my wall.

Zach walked over to me and tightly wrapped his arms around my waist.

He kissed the top of my head and breathed down my back. "It's not just because of you, it's because of him. He isn't allowed to talk about me or my family. Especially my girl."

I whipped around, losing what little patience I had. "What do you mean, *your* girl?"

Zach hadn't officially asked me to go steady with him. Maybe he was going to ask me now. Wait a minute, was that what this was about? Oh, I hoped he would. To be Zach's girlfriend . . . A giggle slipped out. I liked that picture. He would be so cuddly and . . . oops, cuddling typically led to something else. What about *that* with a guy you're going steady with? Kyle always expected more. Back to square one, what would Zach be like?

Zach put his arms around me and then looked down at my face. Our faces were too close; my morals thanked Christy for being there.

"It makes no difference. Listen, all that matters is . . ." He kept his eyes on me and lowered his voice without turning around. "Christy, could you give us some privacy? We'll be out in a minute."

Christy got up and started to vacate the room, saying, "I'll be in the kitchen getting a drink. Take your time."

My bedroom door closed.

He was choosing his words carefully, looking everywhere but at me. Then we locked stares. "Tatum, I know I can trust you with this, you'll keep it quiet. My family is different than most; they're not like yours."

I stepped back against the wall. I swallowed the bile in my throat. "Sure. Whatever you say." This wasn't romantic. What did a family have to do with asking me to go steady?

He took his hand to lift my chin and continued, "Once my family knows who I have chosen, their duty is to protect you like they would any spoken for. Even if she . . . you . . . don't agree. The law, I mean the rule, still applies. Tate, you could hate me, but if I've spoken for you, they have to look after you no matter what."

"What—the—hell? Chosen, *spoken for* who? What? Are you in some kind of stupid gang?" Damn it, he wasn't going to ask me to go steady.

Happiness became apparent on his face. "If you want to call it that. My family doesn't, though."

Just like that, my gut ached. "Zach, tell me everything you can. I need to know what this all means. Are you in a gang or not? And what in god's name did Kyle actually say about us that set you off today?"

He kept his voice down. "He went around saying how you and I had sex out in the parking lot after homecoming. He was graphic about how it supposedly happened alongside my car, making you sound like a cheap whore. It was despicable." The corner of Zach's mouth twitched. "I would never do such a beautiful thing with you on the side of a car, please."

He took a step closer to me, and his voice went softer. "And as far as what 'spoken for' means . . . it's that I'm committed to you, and only you. I mean, no other girl will ever interest me, *ever*. My family practices certain politics." With a swift stroke of his hand, he brushed my bangs out of my eyes. "It began in the early twenties. Gramps was in a tough business back home. He moved here in '39, to the US, to get his family away from that as much as possible."

Wait, that was the year WWII began. How old was his Gramps? Wouldn't they have drafted him? Or did they run from the Germans?

"He has a bum leg. Military didn't want him anyway."

Suppose he'd figured out what I was thinking. "I see."

"Anyway, he's now retired from his old business, for the most part. He still keeps some connections in Italy—you can never leave that business a hundred percent."

Zach took his time looking at my eyes, my lips, my forehead. "So when Gramps arrived, he needed work in the States. He and Grandma Cecilia bought a restaurant on the Hill. We all work for him." He took a breath. "Tatum, no matter what my family thinks or does, I'll love you forever. My commitment is real. If there's one thing Gramps remains firm on, it's commitments. You don't have to give me an answer today, but I would love for you to speak for me too. Think about it. I know you feel something for me. It can't be wishful thinking. Please say it's not."

I pushed myself up against the wall. H-o-l-y shit. *They're old mobsters. Not a gang, you idiot.* He was saying that, right? I wasn't just imagining it. "The Mob?" It came out whispered.

He nodded.

Oh, dear god. Speak for him? What the hell did that mean, speak for him? I spoke *to* him. And not that I wanted to date other people, but I didn't want to be a mobster. Would that make me a mobster? That was actually laughable. Me, a mobster. All I wanted was for him to ask me to go steady. He wanted to marry me. A commitment forever? That sounded like a fricking marriage. Lord, my head was killing me.

Not sure why I thought putting my hand on my forehead would make me feel better, because it didn't. Why couldn't he be a normal guy and ask me to take his promise ring? Why the Mob?

Zach lowered his chin, but raised his eyebrows—waiting.

If he was an old mobster's grandson, then why in god's name was I so comfortable with him? That would make anyone in their right mind afraid of him. All right, what was the one thing I knew about mobster families? Once you were in, you didn't walk back out. Shit.

He was giving me time to think, so I needed to think.

His face was begging for approval, and my heart was wringing out to dry.

I met his eyes. "You're my friend, right?" Since he wouldn't be a normal guy and ask me to go fricking steady with him.

"Of course. I think I proved that a long time ago," he responded.

"Then, thank you for protecting my name."

Zach seemed to get the wrong impression. Or maybe it was my stupid choice of words. He picked me up and gently placed me on my bed, crawling over me.

"*Zach,*" I said in a warning tone.

"*Tate,*" Zach said in his wanting tone.

It was completely insane how fast he was moving our relationship.

He slowly kissed my face all over. Feeling his lips mush against different parts of my face made me quiver. With barely an inch between us, he stared me in the eyes, and I stared at him. His eyes told me he was asking permission. I wasn't sure about anything in that moment, but I convinced myself that a kiss of thanks was in order. He did protect my honor.

A little tug on his neck sent him to my lips.

On contact, my body relaxed. Warm. Soft. Zach knew how to kiss a girl.

As he moved his head from my right side to my left side, kissing, my breathing amplified. My body wanted more. There was one thing on my mind—to have him make me feel better by the second. I'd lost control over my limbs, starting with my legs. They wrapped around Zach. This meant trouble.

Without thinking, I called out, "Christy."

Zach froze, then put his face back to mine. "Are you okay?"

"Yeah, Zach. I . . . I just can't do this right now. Sorry."

"I understand. It's your choice." Zach gave the tip of my nose a quick kiss. "I would never force you to do anything."

We heard footsteps approaching the door. Zach flipped himself over to the side. I got up and straightened my clothes.

Christy inched through the door. "So, everything is settled, then?"

I patted her shoulder. "Yep, everything is good, for now."

As I walked over to my dresser to fix my hair, I noticed Zach roll his eyes. Yep, because I sure as hell wasn't getting into *spoken for*s any further. Not to mention, she had to save me. No way was I going to get involved like that right now. I couldn't trust myself with him.

I looked over at my clock and saw an hour had gone by since Zach had called me over.

Zach followed my actions. "Well, I guess I better get going. I need to go home and shower before we go down to the Hill."

"The Hill, you mean your Grandpa's place?"

Zach stepped up to me. "Yeah, remember two weeks ago when I was going to ask you to do something with me on that Friday night?"

"Oh yeah, when you pouted because Andi asked me first?"

He stroked his hand down my arm. "Yeah, that's when. Well, anyway, I was going to invite you to go down there with me so I could introduce you to the rest of my family."

His family? They were mobsters. Oh, hell no. I wasn't going there.

"Tate, you're my love, remember?"

"Yes, you remind me every frickin' minute. You won't let me forget."

Zach laughed, pushing me up against the wall.

I squirmed, "Zach, please."

He kissed me, then backed away from my lips. "See you in the morning."

I nodded.

Christy and I led him to the front door. He hugged me goodbye. This was becoming too comfortable a habit. A dangerous habit.

I rolled my eyes toward Chris, who was looking uncomfortable.

Zach winked at me and stepped over to Chris and gave her a goodbye hug and a kiss on her cheek. Her mouth fell open as she placed her hand where he'd kissed. I knew how that felt, soft and warm.

Zach waved goodbye from his car before taking off.

I turned and closed the door. In my bedroom, we both collapsed on the bed.

I hardly heard Christy's chatter. I had a lot to think about.

CHAPTER 23

November 1989

Walking into school the next morning, I wasn't sure what kind of mood I was in. I was "spoken for" by a Mob grandson, which was either terrifying or kind of cool. I wasn't sure which yet. He was waiting for my answer: would I join him? Laughable. And the Mob guy protecting my honor beat the shit out of my ex. That wasn't so bad, but he could be hauled away by the police soon.

What a fiasco.

So when Diane caught me in the hall, I wasn't the friendliest, which made me mad at myself because Di was one of my best friends and I rarely got to see her.

She walked with me to my locker while ranting about how Kyle was the biggest jerk she'd ever known, and how she'd never liked him. I was taken aback by all the information, including how happy she was that Kyle had gotten exactly what he deserved. My day was starting off great.

I stopped dead in my tracks. "What do you mean, you're glad he got it?"

"Don't you know?" she gasped.

"Know what, Diane?"

"Kyle got beaten up this past weekend. I thought you would have heard."

Oh. Just beaten up. "I did, but what happened to him? I mean, was it bad? And please tell me without saying his name."

Diane chuckled, moving something on the floor with her foot. "Yeah, I believe it was bad. Being an asshole finally caught up to him."

"Then you've seen him?"

"Yeah, in the hall when he arrived this morning. Why are you acting so aggravated, Tate? I thought you would be happy."

How could Zach avoid the authorities?

I had to get to my locker. There had to be something in there that would smack against the floor real loud. "I'm never really happy when someone gets hurt, even if he is a douchebag."

Diane snickered.

What a disgusting word, *douchebag*. Kyle loved using it, so it seemed only fitting to call him that.

Diane increased her pace to keep up with me. "I heard what he was saying about you and Zach Bertano last week. I like Zach. I know he's kind of quiet, but there's something about him. Besides . . . he's the sexiest guy in school."

The last thing I needed reminding of—his sex appeal. "So, was there anything wrong with the Football Player?"

Diane's shoulders adjusted. "Oh yeah, he had a big cut across his cheek and it's bruised real bad. Then a big sling that's cramping his jersey."

So it was obvious someone beat the crap out of Kyle. *Gosh darn it, Zach.* How was he going to hide from the police?

It was no surprise that Zach was waiting at my locker for me in his usual stance. Andi was already talking to him, but she stopped to greet me, then excused herself till lunch.

I got into my locker with Diane still there. I said, "Zach, you know Diane, right?"

"Di," was all he said.

He leaned over, giving me a quick kiss on the side of my head.

Di looked up at him and had that same gleeful sparkle in her eyes, just like Andi now did, and Christy after he'd hugged and kissed her.

"So, Zach, guess what Diane just told me?"

He didn't say anything. Just glared at me, a little unsure of what I was getting at.

"Well, I'll tell ya." I spat while reaching for my folder and notebook for first hour. "Diane here said it looks like someone beat the crap out of the Football Player. His arm's in a sling and there's a big gash across his cheek." I slammed my locker shut, exactly the loud noise I wanted. That felt good. "So. Whatcha think about that?"

Diane bit her lip. "I think I'll talk to you later, Tate. See ya." And she was gone.

I moved in closer to Zach, who was still leaning up against the locker next to mine. "So, I'm waiting . . . what do you think about that?" I got right up to him.

Zach smiled from ear to ear. "Think it sounds as if he got everything he deserved."

"I just don't see how you're going to avoid getting in trouble, Zach. You sent him to the fricking hospital, for Christ's sake. People talk." How can people do such damage and not get in trouble? Not possible.

He gently placed his warm hand on my cheek and turned my face up to his. "I won't. Please don't worry. I swear to you, I won't even hear about it." Once our eyes met, he seemed to realize something. "Besides, he knows I'd kill him if he tells anyone."

Not what I'd hoped to hear. "Ugh. Boys." I'd had enough.

"Tate? Come here. Come on, sweetie. Don't be like that." He ran after me.

Third hour came, and I still hadn't spoken to Zach since that morning.

As usual, I stepped off to the side and waited to talk to him. "Do you know how uncomfortable this is going to be for me? Could you possibly have any clue what hell I'm going to experience with *him* in there under these circumstances?"

He encased me with his body and bent his face to mine. "Tatum, if he says one word to you—"

"Yeah, I get it, he'll have to answer to you. I'll see you after class." I ducked under his arm and headed inside the classroom. I didn't look at anyone else, not even Eric behind me.

Eric leaned forward and whispered, "You okay?"

I waved and popped my hand to him without turning around.

He leaned back into my hair again. "So Tate, did you see Kyle?"

I shook my head.

"He got in a fight this weekend."

I whispered back, "I know."

"Do you know with whom? No one seems to know what happened."

Being discreet was a must. I kept my face from everyone's view for fear my eyes would give what I knew away. I gently shook my head, again.

The bell rang fifty minutes later and as usual, I waited for my tall Italian. Most of the kids vacated, following the teacher out, except for a few of us.

Eric came behind me and whispered, "He's still back there. Be careful."

I looked up at him and mouthed, "Thanks." Then Eric walked away, only looking back at me once with apprehensive eyes. I had to be ready for when Zach arrived. He rarely took that long to get to my class after the bell. The one time he must have gotten caught up, I was left with Kyle, alone.

There were footsteps coming up behind me. I held my breath. It came down to this.

Kyle stood next to me. I noticed the white sling. He was so close I could have touched him. *Don't panic, just breathe. What can he do here in school? He can't hurt you. He wouldn't think of it with Zach around. Somewhere.*

"So, your boyfriend doesn't like hearing that you're not a virgin anymore? That really seemed to piss him off when I told him that *I* was your first."

I can't breathe. He didn't? He wouldn't.

I felt that weight on my chest again. Tears were inevitable. A crippling feeling gushed over me like a volcano erupting. *My back burned from being thrust back and forth on the carpet. No. This stops now. He can't cripple me anymore. I won't let him.*

I growled. "You raped me. I've done nothing to you, but I will if you don't leave me the hell alone."

"Leave you alone? You love this attention, don't you? You go from one guy to the next without letting your legs come back together in between. He can have—"

Whatever had kept me in that seat thus far left. Just like that, everything I'd kept bottled up exploded from within. I leaped to my feet. With a bunch of saliva in my mouth, I spat it square in his face. "Why don't you go find Bonnie? I'm sure she'll be wondering why you're not up her ass."

Kyle's face was beet red. I had to hurry.

I grabbed my stuff and ran past him in a panic. I could hear him right behind me just when Zach walked in the doorway. Reaching out for Zach's arm and giving it a yank, I pulled him to my locker.

"Tatum, what did you do? Why are you crying?"

At my locker I started to laugh while shaking violently. It was impossible to do my combination. "I told Asshole Kyle off and spit in his face."

Once my locker was open, I wiped away the tears. Zach was quiet. I threw my stuff inside and turned around to him.

He couldn't smile any wider. "You did?"

"Yeah, I did. Now he's pissed." Then I told Zach everything I'd said, minus one thing.

Zach grabbed me and laid a big kiss on my lips and laughed. He held my shoulders. "Ah, Tate, you made my day."

"I did?"

"Of course, but why are you shaking?"

Was it that visible to others? I looked down and it wasn't that bad. "Well, when I get real scared or real mad, or even both, I shake."

He grabbed my hand and walked me down the hall. "Calm down, Tate. Everything is fine. You'll never have to worry about him, or anything else, for that matter, as long as I'm around."

Made-to-order comfort.

Zach was everything I'd hoped for in a boyfriend—if he'd at least ask me to go steady. How did I get so lucky with him? His eyes were dark with an intensity that showed he meant what he said. And in those long, masculine arms, nothing scared me. He was right. Nothing to worry about.

When we arrived at lunch, walking hand in hand down the main stairway to the cafeteria floor, I noticed more people watching us than usual. I squeezed Zach's hand to let him know he was to hold me. But Zach decided my hand wasn't good enough; instead he grabbed my waist and pulled me close to him.

*****

Zach's three friends came by the table near the end of our lunch break. It was shocking to see Tyler's nose for the first time. He had a huge gash across the bridge of it, and his glasses were gone. All three took a seat around our table. Andi was about to pee herself, giving Matt, who sat next to her, goo-goo eyes.

"Tyler, are you going to be okay?" I asked.

"Ah, sure, Tate. This here"—he pointed to his nose—"this is nothing. I've had worse."

"Your glasses, though?"

Zach grabbed my hand and put it to his lips. "Tyler's fine."

I noticed, even in my confused state, that Bobby had his middle finger in a splint. I was sure it hurt, and yet his smile never diminished.

The two-minute bell rang. I said bye to Andi and noticed Matt checking out her chest.

I cleared my throat and told Andi bye, and she quickly stood to give me a hug. I whispered in her ear. "Andi, he's not what you think."

Luckily she let it go with just a quizzical expression.

The moment the front door lock unlatched, the phone began ringing. I darted for my bedroom phone. "Tate, I wanna hear what you meant at lunch about 'he's not what you think.'"

"I can't say exactly. But are you interested in Matt?"

"Yeah, did you see the way he was looking at me? I like how tall he is. I wouldn't feel so self-conscious around him. Yeah, I guess you can say I'm pretty interested. Wait, why? Did he say something about me?"

"No, but I saw how he was looking at you. You know where he was looking, right?"

"Sure, my chest."

"*Aaannnd*, that's okay with you?"

"I suppose. Most guys look there first."

I chuckled. "You're right about that!"

Poor Andi, she was not of normal size in the bust area. She and Matt could be a good match—they weren't petite people. Matt was so big he could probably throw me across the football field. Well, maybe that was overdoing it somewhat.

"Okay, then, here's the deal, Andi. If you choose to make it known you're interested in this guy, and you two get as far as dating each other, my fair warning to you is that you may not get out as easy as a typical breakup. Before it gets to that point, please make sure you want him, and for a long time." I wasn't sure if Andi could handle a forever.

"Tatum Duncan, what in god's name are you going on about? You make it sound as if we would be exchanging blood."

Hmm, that's curious. I wonder?

CHAPTER 24

It was about four o'clock when I heard the rumbling sound in front of the house. I looked out and Zach was walking up to the house carrying a large food tray. He'd brought food? He always seemed to surprise me. Toni came running from the kitchen. When she saw him, she bounced like a rabbit. I stood with one hand on the door and one hand ready to keep Toni from getting in Zach's way.

"Is it Zachy, Sis?"

"Yeah, Tone, it's *Zachy*," I said, loud enough for him to hear.

He started chuckling, amused with little Toni.

"What did she just call me?"

"Zachy." I looked down at her. "Now Toni, back up so Zachy can get in the door."

Zach would not be happy with me if I didn't let him give his entry fee. So I assumed the position with one cheek turned upward for him. I always felt better after he kissed my face. Toni ran into the kitchen and down to the basement steps, yelling, "Britt, Zachy's here. Come up."

I ran after her. "No, Toni, don't put him on the spot like that. You go downstairs and play with Brittany till Mom and Dad get home."

She gave me a sad look and made her friend, turn around and go back downstairs, mumbling, "No, she's making us stay down here. I wanna play with him, though."

I went back into the living room, where Zach stood holding a huge caterer's-size covered aluminum pan.

"Sorry about that. So what's this?" I said.

"It's from my family's place down on the Hill. It's for your family."

"Why?"

Zach looked taken aback. "Why not? It's just a pan of lasagna. It's my way of introducing myself properly to your parents, especially your father."

In that moment, my nerves ached. What guy is eager to meet a girl's parents, especially the girl's father? He needed to know my dad used to be a boxer. "Oh, well, I'm sure my mom and dad will appreciate it. Do you want to bring it into the kitchen?"

When my parents got home, Zach and I were sitting on the couch, talking.

I stood up. "Um, Zach here brought something for our dinner tonight."

Mom looked confused, and Dad looked skeptical.

Zach stood up next to me. "Yes, Mr. and Mrs. Duncan, I wanted to formally introduce myself. I hope you don't mind, I brought a little something for dinner. It's lasagna from my family's place."

Mom looked like she was ready to sign the marriage license. Dad looked pleasantly taken aback.

Mom spoke first, moving us into the kitchen. "Sure. That's very thoughtful of you."

I walked over to the pan and pointed it out like a "The Price is Right" girl.

Dad's mouth dropped open. "Wow, that's a lot of lasagna."

Mom asked, "Does it need heating up?"

"It may need some, but just a heat-up is all," Zach replied.

"Mom, I already turned the oven on. It should be hot now."

"Thanks." Mom was so happy. For once she didn't have to worry about dinner, and Dad was pleased he didn't have to pay for it—someone else had brought the bacon home.

We all sat for dinner, and luckily the conversation was light. Zach's family's lasagna was delicious. The five of us sat around our small round table.

Dad spoke in between bites. "So Zach, you say this is from your family's place, do they own a restaurant?"

Zach was never more at ease. "Sort of. It's my grandparents' place, Bertano's on the Hill. The rest of my family work there, though. My parents work during the week, and then for the weekends they rotate with my two uncles and their families. Last week was our turn."

Dad talked with food on the inside of his chipmunk cheeks. "I had an uncle who worked down there in the forties." He swallowed. "But he went missing. Up and disappeared. Uncle Phil never said what he did, for who . . ."

Zach hunched his back with his shoulders up and avoided eye contact with me and my family. No one seemed to notice but me. Dad was in his own world, speaking about Great Uncle Phil. And to be honest, although I liked to talk about and remember family members and their stories, Zach's behavior was more interesting. It was tempting to nudge him with my foot under the table to see how he'd respond.

"Kenny, let's change the subject, it's dinner," Mother said.

"Yeah, sure." Dad dabbed at his mouth with a napkin. "So I take it you're Italian, Zach?"

I muttered, "Dad."

Zach sat back up and reached under the table and patted my leg in an *it's okay* way. *Crap, I think Mom noticed.*

Zach moved his hand back on top of the table. "Yes, sir, we're one hundred percent Italian."

"Hmm. And your religion?"

"Kenny, I don't think that's important," Mom interrupted. Thank god. "It's okay, Mrs. Duncan. We're all Catholic, sir."

Dad mumbled, shoving another bite in his mouth. "Well, Tate's grandmother would have been happy."

Would Grandma really have approved?

"So what nationality are you, sir? I mean, with a name like Duncan, you would think Scottish."

"Well, Zach, you would think, but I'm pure German, and Cynthia is half German, half Scottish. My grandparents on my father's side came over and changed our German name to a more Scottish-sounding one."

Zach stopped eating. "Why did he do that?"

"He didn't. Ellis Island anglicized our German name. Anyhow, that's the story behind our Scottish name. My mom's side is a hundred percent German too. My parents met in church and married before the US got involved in the war. My father was shipped out eleven months later. Zach, what's your last name, son?"

"Bertano, sir. My full name is Zacharia Nicola Bertano."

We all looked at our guest. He said his name in full with an Italian accent. I was slightly surprised. In a good way. "You speak Italian?"

"I was raised speaking Italian, Tate. English is my second language."

"Well, I've never heard your accent before." I took a sip of water.

"I was born here, in the US. Only my grandparents have the strong Italian accents. They came over from a small city called Bologna."

"Oh yes, I've heard of Bologna before. Is it beautiful?" What in the world? Why am I getting giddy with him? Oh, mama. I was playing with fire. I knew why they'd left Bologna.

"Very, Tatum, my family goes back once a year at the holidays. Some of my extended family is still there. Actually, we'll be leaving soon for our annual visit."

"Do you go with all of the family, your grandma and grandpa too?" I asked, gleefully looking into his dark, intense eyes. No clue why I did that.

Zach looked right at me and spoke softly. "I do."

In that split second, his eyes sparkled even more. How could his eyes change like that?

"Hum mhh." Mom and Dad both cleared their throats. *Right, lasagna.* I looked down at my plate. My sister looked around, trying to figure out what had just happened.

Toni smiled like a kid who'd just won an argument. "He likes Sissy . . . a lot."

The whole family became very hungry in that moment.

After dinner, Zach properly excused himself. He stood and asked my parents whether they would have a problem with him taking me out for a while.

I looked at Zach, surprised, but of course going along with it. Dad walked over with his hand out. "Zach, son, it was a pleasure. And tell your family thanks for the lasagna, very thoughtful of you and them."

Mom called from the kitchen. "Thanks, Zach. Don't be late, Tatum. You start work in the morning."

She was always a buzz kill. As if I would forget about starting my new job this weekend. I grabbed my jacket and we were out the door and in his Camaro, going down the street.

Zach parked at St. Ferdinand Park.

I sat there in the dark and glanced around the park. "So, is this what you do? Take your girlfriend's family a good dinner and some conversation, then lead her off so you can have your way with her—with the parents' approval, of course?"

I smiled at Zach. He slid his seat back a bit and unbuckled. He leaned over to me and softly said, "Tatum, you have some sauce around your mouth." He leaned in and brushed it off with the tip of his thumb, then backed away. "It's gone now." His pearly whites were showing. "Why do you look so surprised?"

"I have no clue why you still seem to surprise me." I looked around the park again. "So what are we doing here?"

"We need to talk." Zach's voice turned cold.

I whipped my head around to him, fearing what was coming.

I knew what was coming.

The warm fuzzy feeling was gone.

I started to perspire.

"Tatum, stop shaking, I'm not going to do anything. I really just want to talk."

"About?" I closed my eyes and held my breath.

"About something Asshole said that's been eating me alive."

"Does anyone else know what he said?" I couldn't look at him. I was scared out of my mind. Not of Zach. Of the truth. That was to be my secret.

"Tatum, how do you know what I'm going to say?"

"Remember today when I said I told him off and spit in his face? Well, that's what he was telling me in class, how he flaunted it in your face. And that you didn't like hearing . . ." I swallowed hard, looking down in my lap. "I can't say it, Zach." I noticed he hadn't moved since I'd started speaking. I took a peek at his face.

"Tatum, did you give yourself to him?"

"What? No. No, I didn't."

"Then why does he say different?"

This was ugly. If I'd known this was what he wanted to talk about, I would have stayed home.

He seemed emotionless. "Zach, I'm afraid."

"Afraid of what, Tatum? It's a yes or no answer."

Zach was starting to push me. I didn't want him mad at me, but I didn't think he should upset me either. His arm rested on the steering wheel, his body facing me. I still shook; I couldn't help it. "Um, because I guess he wants to claim it. I don't know." That was everything but yes or no.

"Tatum, how does he know of a birthmark on your body if you two weren't intimate?"

"A birthmark? What? Where?" I was sweating bullets now. There were only two ways that anyone would know of my birthmark. Either I'd told them about it, or they'd seen me naked in frontal view. I couldn't believe Kyle would go to that extreme. *Damn it.* Now I wished Zach had killed him.

"Tatum, how? Because he described a birthmark on your front, right above . . . on your right side, and he said it's shaped like a hummingbird. Unless the asshole lied about that and you don't have a birthmark. Which is it, Tate?"

"It's not what you think."

"This is so simple, Tate. Either you were intimate with him. Or you weren't."

"He's right about the birthmark, yes, but it's not what you think."

Zach turned away for a moment before looking back at me. We were both trying not to lose our tempers.

"Okay, if you have a birthmark, can I see it, then?"

"Huh? What for? Can't you just take my word?" I asked him.

Zach's shoulders went up and then he exhaled. "Look. That asshole shoved a lot of shit in my face, and all I'm asking are simple questions. If he wants to shove it in my face again, then I can confidently shove back that I've seen it. I'm not asking to be intimate."

He had a talent for making his requests sound reasonable. So I reclined my seat so it would be easier to control what I showed. I jerked one arm out of a sleeve, then the other, before slapping my jacket down on the floor. Then I slowly pulled my skirt and undies down to just right above.

He examined my birthmark.

His chest pumped.

He looked me square in the face.

I backed up, away from him.

"Kyle described it perfectly." Zach squeezed his eyes shut. "You're not telling me something. If you didn't have sex with him, then how in the hell does he know about that birthmark?" Zach opened his eyes and began raking his fingers across the steering wheel. I could see his chest pumping up and down. He was going to blow. Then a growl came from his direction. "Tatum, tell me now. This dance is over."

I thought I might be sick to my stomach. My nervous shakes intensified. To help, I tucked my hands in between my legs.

"*Tatum,*" he demanded.

"He fucking raped me. That's how he knows about my birthmark. He stole my virginity," I cried out, then threw my face in my hands. I didn't mean to tell him that much.

Zach clicked that key with such force I thought it would snap off in the ignition. "He's dead," Zach growled.

He shoved the shifter into gear and we peeled out of the park. I sat back and closed my eyes, not understanding why my shitty life turned into a constant suicide mission.

"Zach, what are you doing? Where are you taking me?"

"Tyler's house." Zach didn't take his eyes off the road.

Why his friend's house? "No, Zach, please. Listen, this was right when school started. You and I weren't together then."

Zach became more outraged with each word, testing the car and its abilities.

Luckily, we didn't have far to go. Apparently Tyler lived in the nice, new neighborhood of Forest Chase Estates. We pulled into the driveway of an enormous, beautiful two-story brick house with a three-car attached garage. The house was lit with professional landscape lighting. The picture of normal.

Zach shifted down, slammed on the brakes, and yanked up the parking brake. He flew out of the car, then opened my door and took my arm. With a soft voice he asked, "Please, Tate, come with me."

Even though my hands were dripping sweat and I couldn't breathe, I took his hand. And for some reason, I knew Zach wouldn't hurt me.

Tyler opened the door before we got up to it and stepped to the side so we could pass him. Zach was pulling me along.

Tyler raised one eyebrow to me. "Tatum."

Like my dog would, I tilted my head to the side.

We went into one of the smaller open rooms on the left side of the foyer, in the front of the house. Zach walked me into an open room off to the left side. He dropped my arm and pointed to the white couch in the sitting room. "Sit down."

I slapped my hands on my hips. "You're not going to talk to me like that. How dare you?" I bugged my eyes out. Zach paced the room, completely ignoring me.

Tyler came in. "So I see you talked to her."

"Yeah, but it's not what we thought." Zach's right arm flew around when he said that. I'd never seen him so irate.

Tyler sat down in the matching white armchair next to the couch. "So what is it, then?" He was completely calm.

I sat down on the edge of the couch. I was appalled that they were talking about me as if I weren't there.

Zach stopped his pacing and faced Tyler. "He raped her. That's how that fuck knows about the birthmark. He raped her when school started back up again."

Oh shit, Zach, you didn't. How could he just blab it out like that?

Zach froze where he stood. He slowly turned his head to me. He walked over and collapsed to his knees and dropped his head in my lap. "Tatum, I'm so sorry I couldn't save you. He needs to pay for this." Zach then put his arms around me and hugged. His face was down in my lap, which was the least of my worries.

I rubbed Zach's short black hair. "Zach, this is exactly one of the things I was afraid of. This is also one of the reasons why no one is to know. I want to be left alone, and I want him to leave me alone. If you keep confronting him, you'll only make it worse. And not to mention, I want this kept quiet. Zach, please, I beg you. It's more important to me to keep this quiet. Please act as if you never asked, and I never told you. Promise me."

I forgot Tyler was there for a moment when he said, "She's right. We're not going to touch Kyle for this. Especially since he did it before you spoke for Tatum. And we'll honor her request that no one shall know about the rape."

What the heck was going on with them? Why were they still talking like this? Wait. Was this his family? "Okay, can you guys please stop saying that word? It makes me uncomfortable."

Tyler nodded. "Of course, sorry."

Zach took his head out of my lap and looked up at me, saying, "Sorry. I won't say it again. I understand."

Zach needed more than us in each other's arms, he needed our lips touching, and his lips took mine.

CHAPTER 25

We heard footsteps in the house. Bobby and Matt walked into the room from the back of the house.

I didn't take my eyes off the boys when I asked Zach to slide up on the couch next to me.

Bobby looked taken aback and put his hands on his hips. He turned to Zach. "What's going on, cousin?"

Tyler was still sitting there as calm as a turtle. "Zach talked to Tatum."

"I see, so the birthmark and everything?" Bobby said, lifting his eyebrows.

What the hell? Do they all fricking know? Kyle. His big mouth . . . eww, that asshole.

Zach sat next to me, not saying a word. He started to rub my knee. To say that I was embarrassed that they all knew about me and Kyle was the understatement of the year.

"Yes, but it's not like Kyle made it out to be," Tyler said. "They need to know."

Exactly why I hadn't wanted *anyone* to know, because now everyone did.

Zach and I gave a nod.

Tyler moved this time and rested his arms on his knees, looking more casual. Not taking his eyes off of Zach, Tyler said, "This never leaves the room," and waved his finger. The boys nodded. "But Asshole raped Tatum."

In unison, Bobby and Matt took a sizable step back.

Zach took my hand. "The point is, is that *asshole* made it sound like something other than what it was. And now Tyler and Tatum have decided to do *nothing*."

I squeezed Zach's hand, with all eyes still on me.

Matt and Bobby took the same step forward this time.

Tyler's eyebrows rose, carefully examining me and Zach. "It's the right thing to do, Zach. Like Tate said, she wants to forget about it. Let her."

Zach leapt to his feet. "You wouldn't say that about Bonita if she was ra—I mean, if that happened to her," he shouted.

I could feel my face burning. This was not the place to be discussing what had happened to me. I leaped to my feet. "I wanna go home, Zach. Right now."

He turned to me and put his hands on my hips. The other three guys looked at each other in silence. I made sure to watch all of them.

"I'll take you home," Zach said, then pulled me into his chest.

I tucked my head to hide from their watching eyes. Zach backed up and took my hand and led me out of the room, toward the front door. As much as I liked him wrapped around me, I wanted out of there more.

No one said a word.

At the car, Zach closed my door. That's when I noticed Matt was jogging toward us.

He bent down in my window and handed me a piece of paper. "Tate, do you think you could give this to your friend Andi for me?"

I was surprised but took the envelope. "Sure, Matt, any message or just the envelope?" Matt was lucky he hadn't upset me like Tyler had.

He thought about it for a minute. "Yeah. Tell her . . . I would be honored."

"Um, okay, that's it?"

"Yes, Tatum, thank you," Matt stood up.

"I'll have to give it to her Monday. I work all weekend," I said to Matt.

He nodded in return and Zach pulled away.

"So, do you know what this is about?" I waved the envelope at Zach.

"Yep."

"Okay, would you like to elaborate a little?"

"I would like to, but I can't."

"You and your stupid laws. Excuse me, *rules*."

Zach looked at me and laughed. "Don't let my family hear you call them stupid."

"Whatever," I mumbled.

I turned in my seat to face him. "And would you like to tell me why they were all there? They aren't just your friends. Bobby called you 'cousin.'"

"Yeah. They're my cousins. Tyler is the first one, then Bob. I'm the youngest." He took his eyes off the road and turned to me. "Like I said, we're family."

Zach pulled up in front of my house and pulled up the parking brake.

This was it; he probably wouldn't want to see me again. There was no way a guy would let this go, let alone Zach Bertano—grandson to Mr. Old Mobster. I was sure to get his eviction notice.

Zach looked at me and said slowly and softly, "Tatum, *ti amo cosi tanto.*"

Jesus. That was one sexy eviction notice.

I had no clue what he'd said, except that the first word was my name. "Zach, I'm sorry. Could you speak English for my sake?"

"Tatum, I love you so much. That's what I said."

He loved me? He wasn't breaking up with me over this. It's confirming what I'd felt from the beginning. Just thinking about Zach made me giddy inside, but in his presence, my chest ached from the pounding of my heart. And this ache for his love was only getting worse.

My gut told me to look away, so I did. Then I felt his hand on my cheek and I turned back to him. Approval was spelled out all over his face. I had never been in love before, so this feeling was new to me. But I knew that I loved this guy. But . . . what was *my* problem? Embarrassment. The whole stupid Kyle thing was an embarrassment to me. Not only did Zach know, but his cousins did, too. "Thanks, Zach."

"Thanks?" Zach's smile faded. He paused and tightened his lips. "You're right. It's your choice."

What was I to say? I made the moment uncomfortable between us.

He wouldn't look at me. "I would never force you to do anything, Tatum . . . that you didn't want to do."

Why was it when a guy was nice and not pushy, I wanted to change my mind and give in to them? Was it guilt? Love? Who knew, but I surely didn't want to hurt his feelings.

With his hand still on my cheek, I cupped my hand over his. That's all it took to make us both happy. Seconds went by with neither of us moving.

Zach wasn't going anywhere. *This is stupid of me. Why fight what I want? He's never shown anything besides commitment to me.* It was time to let my reservations go. I exhaled, and that was Zach's okay.

His other hand cradled my other cheek and he lowered his head to mine. Our lips were ready. I balanced on the console for leverage to kiss him. His hands dropped from my face, and then his seat reclined. He grabbed my arm and in one swift motion, I was on his side, draped over him. Making out became more and more comfortable, until I feared we would continue to push to the next step.

Feeling like a pro, I sat up on Zach, straddling him—actually, it was my second time, but I wasn't counting.

With droopy eyes, he asked, "You okay, hon?" Zach pushed up on his elbows.

"I have a question."

"Ookaay." He dragged it out.

"If I do speak for you, what does that mean for us?" I tilted my head. "Sex?"

"Well, I guess, yeah. Spoken for, Tate, is our way of committing forever without marriage."

"So we wouldn't marry?"

He chuckled, "Not now, but in years, sure."

I glanced out his window. Going to bed with anyone was an intimidating thought. He would see me naked. Of course, I would get to see him naked. I wasn't ready for that.

Again, he guided my face back to his. "Hon?"

I turned my head farther and kissed the palm of his hand. I could feel his body react.

"I better go in. It's getting late, Zach."

I went to fall back into my seat, but he stopped me. I looked at him. "Yes?"

"Just a goodnight kiss?" Zach asked.

I settled back on him. "Right. You're funny."

Bending back down to him, I placed my hands on his head rest and kissed his lips.

He embraced me with a gentle caress on my back. His lips were nothing short of amazing, and soft. Zach was a great kisser.

He held me on top of him. "I know you just asked about 'speaking for' and what it means in other ways. Like in the future. Guess that means you haven't made a decision. Have you even thought about it?"

Right. I owed him an answer. *That's actually all I think about. Would I speak for him or not? Guess he wants my answer now.* "Ummm—"

"Don't worry. I think I should take a different approach."

"What? Different . . . different approach?" He reached down for my hands. That made-to-order comfort was back. Zach seemed to know how he affected me. He brought my hands up to his lips. His intense eyes looked through me. Everything would always be fine with him around; Zach had that written all over his face.

"Yes, I should have approached you about this differently. You may understand this better if I approach it this way."

He clearly loved mind games. I had no clue what he was talking about.

Zach's signature smirk was back while he drew each of my fingers up to his mouth and kissed, slowly, gently mushed against his warm lips.

I glanced over at the window, wishing it was cracked for a breeze to cool things off a bit. It felt like the heater was on maximum power.

After each finger was kissed, he held still. "Tatum, instead of asking if you'll speak for me, how about I ask you to go steady with me? Will you be my girlfriend?"

He did it! He finally asked me to go steady! Me . . . Tatum Duncan . . . officially Zach Bertano's girlfriend! This I can handle.

"Yes! Of course. Of course I'll be your girlfriend!"

We fell against each other.

An hour before, I'd thought he wouldn't want me once he knew about my virginity, or lack thereof. But he did. Zach clearly loved me. He'd protected my name. Even with terrible baggage like mine, he still wanted to be with me. No one else mattered to him. He would be there for me. I was lucky to have such a boyfriend. Zach was one in a million. And maybe it wasn't so bad that his family was different from most. It just meant we would be more dedicated to each other, something I'd prefer in my life. What more could a girl ask for?

Zach's hands tousled my hair. To make things fair, I did the same to his.

"Zach?"

He stopped toying with my hair.

"I'm so happy. Call me when you get home, before bed? Please?"

The inside of his mouth was pulled inward. "You want me to call you when I get to bed?"

"Yes. Is that okay?" He flopped his head back. "Dear god, if I've died, don't wake me up."

He was too darn cute not to kiss goodnight. Moments later, I grabbed my purse and tossed it over my shoulder. "Goodnight . . . *boyfriend.*"

That sounded perfect.

Zach didn't argue when I climbed off of him and dropped into my seat. Instead, he got out and ran around the outside of the car and opened my door.

"Wait, wait, I have it. Here." He put his hand out for me.

This was right. Zach felt right. I gave him my hand.

Outside, the sky was cloudless with tons of stars. "It's beautiful out tonight." The moon gave us ample light.

His hands cupped my waist. "It is. It's perfect."

Everything was at peace. There was nothing but happiness to look forward to.

NOW ENJOY A SNEAK PEEK AT BOOK 2, GIRL DIVIDED TWO

CHAPTER 1

Tatum

Ten months ago, I had this perfect vision of being a "normal" teenager—what a joke. Of course, at this point, it would be hard to wish certain things didn't happen. Because what I have now, the guy of my dreams, was the result of it all.

Zacharia Nichola Bertano asked me to be his girlfriend three weeks ago.

Who's lucky enough to already have their dream guy as a junior in high school? Me. I envision myself with him for the rest of my life. Of course, that means I'd have to marry the Mob. Yup, the best guy any girl could wish for just so happens to be the grandson of an *ex*-Mob boss from Italy. For now, I'm ignoring that minor hiccup.

Except that I owed Zach an answer to a larger question than whether I'd be his girlfriend—would I "speak for" him?

"Speak for"—that's committing to Zach without the ring on my finger, which isn't a problem, but I'd have to commit to his family, too. A Mob family. This was not a decision to take lightly. I was worried enough about that, but Zach also wanted me to meet his grandfather and his parents over the weekend.

Can you see me, a girl who wears black combat boots with miniskirts and has the side of her head shaved, walking up to Mr. Ex-Mobster with my hand out? *Hello, Mr. Mobster Grandpa, I'm Tate* (don't tell him your last name)*, it's so nice to finally meet you.*

Who meets a mobster . . . *ever*? Zach says he's been out of the business since they moved to St. Louis, but I'm no idiot—once you're in the Mob, you don't walk back out. I've seen *The Godfather*—twice.

Zach

Sometimes I hated being me, Zach Bertano. My family was a pain in the ass. We weren't the normal family. We were Mob . . . kind of. Gramps was an old-time Mob boss with one foot in the past and one in the here and now. It was his past that was causing me problems, because I was in love with Tatum Duncan. It only took me three years to become her boyfriend.

Tatum wasn't a girl you walked up to and started chatting with. But even before we'd ever really talked, I could see her strength and determination in those guarded eyes. Whether she knew it or not, she had qualities that would fit right in with my family.

In school Tatum sat next to me at our lunch table. She and Andrea, who was dating my cousin Matt, were talking as usual while eating. Tatum was so beautiful. If only she'd realize how I would go to the end of the earth for her. But to rush her into an answer would kill my chances. That's why she was clueless about the pressure my Gramps had been putting on me for the past month to get her to "speak for" me in return.

Gramps didn't accept the "just dating" commitment Tatum preferred. Gramps was old school—you commit, she commits, end of story. And no matter if my father was Lead Man and my mother was Lead Woman here in the US. Gramps overrules everyone, even my uncle Vito back in Italy. The only thing my parents could do for me was help stall. Tatum needed more time. Ironic how similar Gramps and Tatum were. Stubborn. Pig-headed. Determined.

Once the school bell rang, announcing the end of lunch, I walked Tatum to her fifth hour, which was close to mine. Since her ex-boyfriend couldn't be trusted, I insisted on walking her to every class.

I walked into the boys' locker room and went to my usual locker of choice in the back corner. The back corner was usually quiet by now with the previous class gone, but not today. There was chatter coming from the row on the other side of the lockers. I only listened in because I noticed his voice.

That fucking voice sent a charged nerve down my spine. Kyle Wilson. Tatum's ex-boyfriend.

The jock who had to date her.

The jock who cheated on her.

The jock who raped her.

"That bitch walks around here with her nose up in the air with that fucking lowlife Italian's hands all over her. People only know Tatum because *I* dated her . . ."

I could feel my hand flexing instinctively from hearing him call her a bitch. *Keep talking, Star*

Football Player, I'll show you what a lowlife Italian I can be.

"She'll still get what she has coming to her," Kyle said.

I glanced around me; no one was on my side of the lockers. I wanted to rush over there and snap Kyle's fucking neck. Because she was the one girl who wouldn't put out, she'd bruised his ego, and he couldn't take it.

The weight of my family's politics weighed on my chest. If Tatum only understood the protection she could get from this asshole if she'd speak for me.

"Kyle, shhh, keep your voice down. You know it echoes in here—"

That was his buddy, Aiden. Fine, I could take him too.

"What do you mean, 'She'll still get what she has coming to her'? You honestly think we're stupid enough to fight the Bertanos again . . . over her? I have a football career to think about. If we get caught fighting, Coach will kick us off the team. You know his policy."

Damn it. It was harder to hear them with more students filing in for the next class. It was a struggle to hear every word.

"Idiot, there's other ways for her to get her due."

"What did Tatum ever do to you, Kyle? Besides, Bertano is with her every waking minute. He threatened to kill you the last time. I'm not sacrificing my football career for anyone, and neither should you," Aiden said.

The sound of a metal locker being caved inward momentarily silenced the locker room. "Big deal, he threatened me. He had to play the tough guy around his cousins. He doesn't scare me. Someway, somehow she'll get what's coming to her. And I won't need anyone's help," Kyle said. "Bertano can't be with her every waking . . . or sleeping moment."

Without thinking, I slammed my fist into the locker, causing the row to vibrate as if they could go down like dominos. The prick was right about one thing. I couldn't be with her every minute, and that really pissed me off.

I threw my gym bag in a locker and stormed around the corner to face Kyle.

I stood there, crossing my arms over my chest. "Whatchya gonna do to Tatum, big bad Kyle?"

Aiden jumped and then took a lunging step back, glancing around. Kyle didn't. He looked pissed that I'd caught him.

I kept my pleasure at startling them to myself. "Do you really think I or anyone in my family will let you within ten feet of her?"

Kyle flung his gym bag to the floor and got in my face. "Do you think you're going to stop me? I'm gonna do whatever I want. *You* don't scare me."

Aiden glanced around again. "Um . . . Kyle, let's go. I'm hungry." He placed his hand over Kyle's shoulder. "I said, let's go."

Kyle jerked his shoulder away from Aiden's hand. "I dare you to touch me again. This fool thinks he intimidates me." Kyle didn't take his eyes off of me, and his face was beet red. Just like Tatum always said, that was a sign Kyle had lost his shit.

A few spectators kept their distance.

I inched forward as far as I could go without touching Kyle and kept my voice down. "I'm going to tell you one time and one time only . . . you lay one of your tiny fingers on her, and I will fucking kill you." He had no clue who he was messing with, even if that was obviously a bluff. I jabbed my finger in his chest. "And so we understand each other . . . my family knows what you did."

Kyle's smug face contorted to panic. Yeah, that got his attention.

"Hey, what's going on here?" Coach Henderson walked up. I respected the Tim Conway lookalike, but I wouldn't let him interfere.

Kyle backed up and snatched his bag from the floor. "Nothing. Aiden and I are going to lunch."

They walked off.

Aiden glanced back at me. Even though Aiden mumbled, I could still hear him. "What is Bertano talking about, Kyle? His family knows what?"

Coach walked toward me. "Bertano? You okay?"

I could feel my chest heaving. "Sure, Coach. Just making sure Mr. Star Football Player knew what I was talking about."

Coach nodded. "Okay." He looked me up and down. "See you out on the floor in two."

No matter what I'd have to do, I'd be damned if I let that asshole touch Tatum again.

ACKNOWLEDGEMENTS

Who doesn't love the saying, "what doesn't kill you will only make you stronger?"

The year my oldest child, my daughter, went off to college, I didn't mope around. I didn't feel sad that she was "gone". I was exhilarated. Relieved. Having a child at the determined age of sixteen years, I dreamt of the day she went to college. Because I never got to. I made my bed. I was damn well lying it in.

After she left for college I felt compelled to write a simple story about how hard it is to be a teenage mom. Once I began, the words and a story came spilling out.

So, to my daughter, for confirming my determination in life. You've made me strong. I know this story would have never blossomed without yours.

To the man who has held my hand from the beginning. The father of my children. It's amazing to me how after twenty six years of being together I love you more.

To my son, the one who makes my life complete. His outward excitement for my books is never hidden from me. Thank you for understanding when I was in my office and you wouldn't interrupt, and then later ask how my writing was going.

I love the three of you!

A special thank you to some of my other family who have not only supported this crazy idea of mine, but helped make my front cover vision a reality: Tiffany Diamond & Leroy Roper. The two of you opened yourselves up to my wishes. You applied body paint to parts we couldn't find the right costuming for. You let me Art Direct the entire photo shoot. We turned on my own playlist for Girl Spoken For and began shooting a beautiful front cover. With your combined (photographer, body artistry, backdrop paintings, model, hair & make-up design) expertise we brought my book to life. Leroy Roper & Tiffany Diamond—Thank you!

Once The Fool, always The Fool!

Thank you so much, Amanda Sumner—my Editor. It's been great working with you on my first book. I'm fortunate to have found such a great editor who isn't afraid to leave funny remarks and who gets my voice. And I'm looking forward to continuing Tatum and Zach's story with you. A special thanks to your son for doing a proofread. It was good hearing from a teenage boy my villain was a jerk. Thanks!

To Zoe Dawson, for taking the time to proofread *Girl Spoken For* without much notice. I greatly appreciate your help.

Thank you, Dana Waganer for not only being a friend, but a great editor. I'm lucky to have a friend who understands and makes herself available. I thank you so much.

Thank you to The Killion Group. Kim & Jen, I can't imagine anyone else being this pleasant to work with. I've loved the work you've produced for me (the front & back cover design, my logo, business cards, bookmarks etc.). You gals are seriously the best. Thank you.

And then there's my brilliant critique group— Linda Gillman, Michelle Sharp & Claudia Shelton. Plain & simple, I would not have gotten this far without you gals. I first met Linda and she asked the rest of the group if I could join them. Even though you gals didn't read YA, except for Michelle, you agreed a YA author could join your already diverse group. The countless phones calls between us for an opinion, or a shoulder to cry on, or to vent, or the happier times of the celebratory calls, you gals are always there. Your help, support and friendship is invaluable.

Thank you everyone!

Suzie

ABOUT THE AUTHOR

Suzie T. Roos is from, and has settled in, St. Louis with her husband, two children and a number of foster pets at any given time. She and her husband have lived everywhere from Philadelphia, PA, to out west in Santa Monica, CA. They're thankful they could expose their children to different American lifestyles and cultures. Besides writing, Suzie's hobbies include movies, traveling, and especially concert going with her husband and friends. She's always been an animal lover and animal rights advocate. She is certified by FEMA in IS-00011.a Animals in Disasters: Community Planning. She's also an active volunteer at the Humane Society of Missouri.

www.suzietroos.com
www.facebook.com/SuzieT.Roos
twitter.com/@suzietroosbooks

CPSIA information can be obtained at www.ICGtesting.com
Printed in the USA
LVOW10s1445211215

467381LV00023BA/1263/P

9 780996 294201